Dying to Build (Nailed It)
(A Tucson Valley Retirement Community Cozy Mystery)
By: Marcy Blesy

This book is a work of fiction. Names, characters, places, and events are a result of the imagination of the author or are used fictitiously. Any resemblance to actual persons, living or dead, businesses, events, or locations is a coincidence.

No part of the text may be reproduced without the written permission of the author, except for brief passages in reviews.

Copyright © 2024 by Marcy Blesy, LLC. All rights reserved.

Cover design by Cormar Covers

Chapter 1

"Hard hat, Rosi! How many times do I have to remind you that you can't be on the construction site without a hard hat? I'm not risking this project's reputation with an accident."

"Sorry, Jakob. I'm really sorry. It's in my car. I'll run and get it," I say, turning to return to my car in the parking lot of the Tucson Valley Senior Center.

"Wait. Take mine. I've got another in the office." Jakob sighs as he takes his hard hat from his head and places it on top of mine where it proceeds to fall forward blocking my vision.

"You'll need to adjust that."

"Thanks, boss," I say, laughing.

"No way! Don't give me the boss title. Way too much responsibility to be the ultimate boss of this project," says Jakob as he sweeps his hands over the area that is quickly becoming the new technology center for the Tucson Valley Retirement Community, with land gifted from Roland Price's will.

"You're a lot friendlier than *the boss*," I say, leaning in with a whisper that sends my hat falling to the ground. "I'll fix it," I say, picking up the hat to adjust the straps.

"I agree, but if that gets out, there will be heck to pay for me and the crew. I've got to get back to work. The lead architect is coming in to go over final plans. I have to prepare."

"Right! Tracy and I will be at that meeting, too. Thanks for the hat, Jakob." I hit the top of my hard hat with my fist and don't feel a thing.

He nods his head and walks back to the trailer that is serving as the main office for the technology center project. His goatee is a deep brown color that matches the thick hair on his head. I don't think he will need to worry about going gray any time soon although with all the worrying he's doing over this fast-moving project, he just might prove me wrong. I still can't believe how fast this center is going up. It's only October, and we broke ground in mid-August. The goal for the ribbon-cutting ceremony is only three weeks away. Though things have moved quickly, there are so many tasks to complete in order to make that deadline. I've been assured by Jakob that we *will be* ready. My confidence in him is so strong that I finalized my printed media this morning with the ceremony date in bold print. I hope that won't prove foolish.

By the time the first snowbirds start to arrive back, the tech center might actually be open and ready for use. What was supposed to be a new job with some fun responsibilities, like handling marketing for the performing arts center and bringing in new acts, has exploded with tasks associated with this new project. Many of the things I'm learning are way over my head, but I love the challenge. Plus, calls to Zak, my uber-talented, techno-loving child have been more frequent. He's a great resource, and I love the excuse to contact him with more specific content-related questions rather than just *hey, I'm lonely and miss my kid* kind of calls.

"Hey, Rosi! Come take a look at this!" I walk toward the young woman with a matching hard hat and a tool belt that could rival a king's, so many shiny tools hanging like fruit for the picking from her hip. I've kind of become obsessed with her badassery.

"Hi, Gabby. What's up?"

Gabby swings her black braid behind her shoulders and takes off her hard hat as she leans close. "Check it out!" she whispers. She points to a spot in the dirt outside of the front door of the tech center which has just been freshly installed.

I walk closer. "Eeeeekkkkkkkkk! Gabby!"

"Shhh… geez, I thought you could handle it. That's why I was whispering. The guys on the crew would go nuts. Just like you, I guess." She shakes her head back and forth as if I've disappointed her. Several of the crew stop what they are doing and stare for a moment, but she dismisses them with her hand and they return to work. "It's only the skin."

"Of what though?" I ask, trying to look braver than I feel.

"A western diamondback rattlesnake. It's a real beauty, that skin is. Almost shed in one perfect piece. Dang, that's pretty." She picks the skin up and holds it in front of my face for me to admire, all three feet of it.

"I'm afraid I don't share your same enthusiasm for snakes, especially the poisonous kind."

"Clearly," Gabby says, depositing the snakeskin into the pile of shovels nearby. "That should give the guys a good jump," she laughs, a deep hearty laugh that's so infectious I can't help but giggle, too.

"Does the skin mean, uh, does it mean that he's still here? Only with new skin?"

"Might just be, Rosi. Better watch yourself."

This time I don't match her enthusiasm.

"Should I bring the skin to book club this week?" An evil glint emanates from her squinted eyes.

"If you do, then you can forget about catching a ride from me!"

She laughs. "If only Caliope Davento wasn't hosting so far out of the city, I'd ride my bike. But that's too far in the evening. Too many crazy drivers on those twisty roads."

"Do you think you'll ever get a car?" I ask my new, unlikely friend whom I'd bonded with over our love for cozy mysteries—her the ones set in bakeries with recipes in the backs of the books and me the ones with cute pups like Barley as sidekicks.

"Nah, no good for the environment. I'll keep using people like you before I add to the pollution in the environment by gettin' a car."

"Glad I could be used. See you later, Gabby. Be careful out here!"

On my way back to the senior center I have to sidestep wheelbarrows, wires, tubing, paint cans, and various other things I've been learning about over the last few weeks, paying close attention for that hidden snake. I'd even gone out and purchased myself a pair of work boots because I grew tired of coming home every day with dirty shoes. I take them off when I get to the senior center, depositing them by the back door next to Tracy's work boots. We'd shopped at the same store.

"Ready for our big meeting?" I ask Tracy as I stop by her office. Her desk is a disaster. File folders, staplers, boxes of more papers, scattered paperclips.

"Does it look like I'm ready?"

"I'm sorry."

"No, I'm sorry," says Tracy, running her hands through her curly hair, getting stuck for a moment, before sighing. "It's just a lot. This project is *a lot.*"

"I know. But remember how excited you were when you talked with Roland Price about the possibilities of this technology center? You were bursting with excitement. Focus on the end game."

"The end game."

"Is there anything I can do to help? I have a meeting with a representative of the Southwest Arizona Senior Dancing with the Starz Competition at 4:00, but I can be available until then."

Tracy smiles. "That sounds so fun. I really hope you decide to bring that competition to Tucson Valley. We have some amazing dancers."

I raise a skeptical eyebrow. "If you say so. My only experience with the dancing of Tucson Valley residents came from '80s theme night at the karaoke bar. Michael Jackson has no competition here."

Tracy giggles. "But what about your famous lift with Keaton?"

I open my eyes widely in surprise.

"Yep, *everyone's* heard about that, Rosi." She laughs. "Anyway, I could use your help. Can you start by helping me organize this mess on my desk? We are supposed to review the final interior design plans before installation: carpets, furnishings, paint colors, finishings, things like that."

"That sounds kind of fun. I'd love to help. I think you should stretch your legs, though. You've been stuck in this office all morning. Go grab us some coffee at Mabel Brown's Café in the sports building, and I'll get started."

"That sounds like a fabulous idea. Thanks, Rosi."

After Tracy has gone, I stand over her desk deciding where to begin. I look longingly at the dog bed that sits empty. Tracy had purchased a dog bed for Barley to use when she'd come to work with me. When I was occupied, Barley would hang out in Tracy's office. However, with all of the extra people and dangerous things like stray nails or wires lying around, I'd decided to put Barley in doggy daycare on the days I couldn't slip home at lunch to take her out to pee. She loves it, of course. I think she's sweet on a cocker spaniel named Grayson. It's a good thing she's been fixed. I don't need the headache of new puppies. I remember back to the litter that Barley was a part of and wonder where they have all gone. My phone dings, snapping me out of my idleness.

Dinner with Oliver?

Yes. But I might meet him before then.

How?

He's on the list of people meeting with Tracy today.

Cool. Looking forward to seeing you later. Smooches.

Heart emoji.

"Everything going well in here?" Mario asks, shaking his head back and forth as he looks at the chaos on Tracy's desk.

"Not really," I say, wrinkling my forehead. "But I'm not helping the situation. I'm texting when I am supposed to be helping to organize."

"You're forgiven."

"Mario, I have a guy question for you, if you don't mind."

Mario holds up his hand. "Oh, boy. If this has to do with the bedroom, I don't want any involvement."

I laugh. "No, it's nothing like that. I'm meeting one of Keaton's old high school friends today. He's an architect working on our technology center project. He's out of Las Vegas."

"That's cool. Meeting the friends. Big step."

I nod my head slowly. "I guess it is."

"Why the sour face, Rosi?" Mario touches my arm gently.

"What if I don't make a good impression?"

"Nonsense! You're awesome. Everyone loves you, Rosi."

"Tell that to Jan and Brenda."

Mario's smile fills his face. "Those old biddies? Don't trouble yourself with the crabby *Karens*."

"Oof! Don't call them *Karens*. That is an insult to *Karen* who is about the sweetest, most mild-mannered woman I've ever met."

"True. My apologies to all of the kind *Karens* of the world. But, seriously, just be yourself."

"Thanks, Mario. I'd better get to work before Tracy comes back."

"Good luck with that mess. I've got my own mess to clean up."

"I imagine it's a pain in the butt keeping up with all of the dust and dirt."

"You have no idea. I'm on my third mop bucket. Ever since they broke ground on our own land—not Mr. Price's—to make room for more parking between our building and the new tech center, the chance of the floors in this building being clean are zero percent." He shakes his head sadly.

"Buck up, Mario. It will all be over in a few weeks—if I can figure out Tracy's organization system!"

"See ya, Rosi. Let me know if you need me."

"I will. Thanks."

I pick up a stack of papers and start reading through them, pulling on my reading glasses to help with the fine print. I make piles: furniture, fixtures, utilities, exterior. One piece of paper marked as *Important* catches my attention. I sit down in Tracy's chair to read.

If this project goes over the spelled-out timeline, the cost per day increases exponentially. The purpose of this project is to offer technology that will enhance the lives of our residents. The increased costs of a late project will decrease the amount of technology we will be able to offer, defeating our project purpose. Your job will be on the line if our project goes over budget. Don't let that happen. You've been warned.

> *Signed,*
> *Brenda Riker, HOA President*
> *Jan Jinkins, Board Member*
> *Bob Horace, Board Member*

I let the paper slip between my fingers back to the desk. No wonder Tracy is a basket case of stress and worry. Her job is on the line. How dare they threaten her when she's worked so hard for this retirement community? And why would Bob have signed his name to such a nasty note? Are those women *that persuasive?*

Chapter 2

At 2:00, Tracy and I walk down the hallway into the performing arts center where a conference table has been assembled on the stage with chairs along both sides, set up by Mario for this special meeting. While the tech center could have handled our presence, there are too many hazards to work around to make the meeting practical there. I squeeze Tracy's hand as we walk into the auditorium as a reminder that she's got this. I carry her now-organized pile of file folders—tabbed and ready to go.

Jakob Beacher, the general contractor, stands up and waves when Tracy and I walk onto the stage. Brent Heath, the construction manager, grunts his greeting without so much as a glance at us. He's looking at his phone and stroking his chin as if deep in thought. I hadn't noticed the roundness of his belly before, but seeing him seated so far away from the table because of his meaty girth makes it kind of hard to miss. The roundness of his body matches the roundness of his balding head. Symmetry. The lead interior designer, a woman named Jade—only Jade—because I'd asked, waves with a smile that lights up her face. "Hello, ladies. Welcome to our meeting." She whips her long blonde hair over her shoulders which she straightens to exhibit the best posture of anyone at the table.

It's really our meeting, I want to say, but I don't. "Hello, Jade."

"Hello, Jakob. And Mr. Heath," I say, trying to remember which of the two men wanted to be addressed by his last name and which one his first name only.

"Greetings," Jakob says as Mr. Heath continues to scroll through his phone.

Members of the HOA board are in attendance, too. Some of my favorite people in the whole wide world. Not.

"Rosi, you didn't tell me that the meeting was casual," Brenda says as she pulls her suit jacket tighter across her chest, her plastic smile on display. She looks me up and down, landing on the tennis shoes I'd changed into when I took off my work boots.

"We are here to talk about a construction project, Brenda. Heels are frowned upon," I say, landing on *her* three inch heeled shoes.

"Hmph."

I used to think that we'd turned over a new leaf in Phoenix when we'd discovered a dead body in my bathtub at the Phoenix Emporium Hotel and Convention Center.

But our honeymoon period of good feelings toward each other had only lasted a few weeks until she lost the mayoral election in Tucson Valley to Leo Lestman. Ever since then, Brenda has been in a perpetual state of disagreement with everyone. Of course, since Mayor Lestman is seated next to Brenda right now, her mood is destined for irritability. I give him a friendly wave anyway.

A man I do not know stands up and holds out his hand for me to shake. "You must be Rosi Laruee," he says, his wide shoulders filling out the ends of his shirt sleeves so tightly that the threads might burst at any moment. He's a very handsome man with piercing blue eyes, two well-balanced dimples, and a thick head of blonde hair.

I realize I am staring and haven't returned his handshake. "Sorry. Yes, I am. Are you Oliver?"

"I am. Keaton's told me so much about you." He winks, and I blush.

"Let's get started," Mr. Heath says as he finally sets down his phone. "I'd like to go over our agenda for the meeting first," he says dryly. "Jakob will present his report about the status of the project. I assume your sub-contractors have given you their reports," he says, looking at Jakob who appears jumpy in his chair, but he nods his head quickly.

"Then we will hear from Oliver, our lead architect, and Jade, our interior designer. Got it?" He looks up, daring us to respond but giving a small smile to Jade who looks away from his glance.

"I have a question," I say, confidently asserting myself. I've had practice with people like this. Plenty of practice. I look at Brenda and take a deep breath. "I would like to guarantee a time for Tracy and me to speak as well. We may have some questions or concerns, too. This is *our* baby—so to speak." Only Oliver is smiling as I assess the people around the table.

"You may ask questions, but we are on a very tight schedule. I can assure you that there are no concerns that you might have that haven't been addressed already. We've had multiple meetings with the board about what they envision this project to be." He looks at Brenda who relishes in his attention. "And Ms. Lake was in those meetings, too." He looks at Tracy who sinks a little lower in her chair.

"I know," I say slowly. "And we appreciate the productivity of those meetings, but things come up. Things change. We want to be included on the agenda for today's meeting should we need to ask questions."

Jakob clears his throat. "Of course, Rosi. Whatever you need to feel heard in this meeting you can have. The technology center is your project." He smiles.

We all jump as Mr. Heath pounds his fist on the table. "We are wasting time. Money is time. No more talking about unnecessary things. Jakob, give your report."

"Sure, Brent...Mr. Heath." He exhales slowly. "Things are moving along nicely. The plumbing is complete. We added extra bathroom facilities per the board's request, with the bathrooms located on each floor for your patrons'...uh, needs."

"That's nice," says Tracy quietly.

"The drywall is done. All the walls are up, of course. The electrical work will be completed by Monday. The exterior painting started yesterday and is nearly halfway done. There is a small part of the exterior shell of the building that we're completing soon."

"What's that?" Mr. Heath interrupts.

"The virtual reality room will be in the round which requires more delicate work than ninety degree angled walls. But I have confidence that we will be ready for the electrician when he arrives on Monday."

I notice that Jakob won't even make eye contact with Brent. He just keeps talking.

"The concrete will be poured for the parking lot and sidewalks in a few days. The only hiccups we've encountered have been staffing problems, like most industries in the United States these days."

"And what are you doing about that?" asks Mr. Heath, squinting his eyes so tightly as he looks at Jakob that his entire face seems to swallow them up, making him look like a pumpkin head.

"Well, I'm the general contractor, so I'm managing the people I've hired, but maybe my construction manager, my boss, can help with the actual hiring process seeing as I'm busy with the day-to-day operation here."

There is a collective sucking in of breath around the table, waiting for Mr. Heath's reply to Jakob's challenge. Mr. Heath is boring a hole in Jakob's head, but Jakob still won't look at him.

"Perhaps we should talk about this matter later. Every second longer this project will take beyond the 30th of October will cost more money."

"To us," I say loudly. "It will cost more money to us."

"And that is unacceptable," adds Brenda.

We are in agreement. It *can* happen.

"Certainly. Oliver, what do you have to add?" Mr. Heath asks, looking at Oliver who stands up and walks to the television that is sitting on a cart at the head of the table.

Hooked up to the television monitor via an HDMI cord, is his laptop. Embarrassing, to say the least, that at a meeting for a state-of-the-art technology center we are going to get a presentation on an old television monitor.

"I can assure you that Jakob is a fabulous general contractor. His communication is top notch. His heart is in the right place. He's doing everything within his means to see this project to a successful completion. The guys—and women—he's hired for his construction crew bust their, uh, butts."

"Go on, Oliver."

"Sure." He pushes a button on his laptop, and the virtual rendering of the Roland Price Technology Center at the Tucson Valley Retirement Community appears on the screen. "The building as you see it today looks very much like it does in this video, near completion. Your concrete teams will be pouring concrete for the sidewalks and parking lots, as Jakob indicated, which will look like this," he says, pointing to the video showing the sidewalks and parking lot outside the building. "There will be a walking path between the senior center and the technology center that will provide both a direct route between the two buildings and also an oval path that, if taken around both buildings, makes for a half mile loop to add exercise opportunities. As I understand it, Keaton and his team will be providing the landscaping for the outside which will look similar to the landscaping in this video—with small hop seed bushes, jojoba bushes, creosote bushes, and San Marcos hibiscus. All of these shrubs are low maintenance, but flowering annuals will be added for color throughout the year. People will come just to see the beautiful landscaping before even setting foot in the tech center. There will be a sprinkler system installed to provide the necessary water for the blue palo verde shade trees, a necessary requirement to help get one through those hot Arizona days. The building has been specifically designed to use the Arizona sun to save on your electric bills. We are installing solar panels on this patch of land. It's better for the environment, too—"

"Hold on a minute," says Mr. Heath. "I don't think we've decided on the landscaping contract yet. You don't get to make that decision unilaterally."

"That's correct," says Brenda. "There are outstanding bids from two other landscaping crews."

"No one will offer a cheaper landscaping package than Keats," says Jade.

Nobody calls Keaton by his nickname but his closest friends. Who does this woman think she is? But I bite my lip, trying not to come across as biased.

"When are the final bids due?" Mr. Heath asks Jakob.

"I thought you were handling those financial issues," Jakob says.

"I am. I am. Let's move on. Oliver?"

"Let me tell you a little bit about some of the technology plans for the center. I've had very productive meetings with Tracy and the board about what technology goals they have prioritized that will fit within their budget and still make Tucson Valley an even more appealing mecca for senior citizens."

I watch Tracy smile at Oliver, and I feel like I missed out on a very cool meeting. There are just too many responsibilities to be everywhere all the time.

"Let's start with the digital art wall."

"Oliver, would you mind if I talked about the wall—since it was my idea and all?" Brenda asks, fluttering her fake eyelashes at Oliver.

Brenda turned seventy one week after I turned forty, but I have to give props to the woman who is fighting mother nature with every last bit of her pocketbook. Mayor Leo and I share a knowing look.

"Go ahead, Brenda."

Brenda stands up and walks to the head of the table. "Thank you, Oliver."

Oliver plays the video and pauses for Brenda to describe the digital graffiti wall where people can interact with the wall by using their fingers to choose colors or patterns or lines to draw and create. It's actually really cool and a great exercise for strengthening fine motor skills in our residents. I don't ask Brenda about that part, though. Brenda curtsies in her fitted black skirt when she is done, and everyone but Mr. Heath claps, even me.

"Thank you, Brenda. The digital graffiti wall is only one of many innovations the tech center will offer. We've also created a voice recording studio for your residents who dabble in song making. The room is nearly complete save for the sound proofing which is coming soon. Then there's the exercise room with exercise bikes that you can program with videos that make you feel as if you are hiking in the Grand Canyon or cycling in the Tour de France."

"We already have a sports center," Mayor Leo interrupts with a look of confusion on his face.

"Leo, this is exercise with technology. Come on now. Even a simple guy like you can understand that," says Brenda.

Oliver clears his throat. "I've created packets that highlight all of the technology features that will be included." He hands yellow folders out to each of us as if he's the teacher and we are his students. "The yellow color is a nod to the awesome color choice for the building."

I can't help but beam like a toddler so that everyone in the room knows who chose the color.

"That's fine," says Mr. Heath. "Jade, your report on the interior finishings?"

Jade brushes her blonde hair over her shoulders and puts on a pair of cat-eye glasses. I wonder if they even have prescriptions or if they are only for show. Perhaps I should update my readers.

"Hello, everyone." She smiles sweetly, but to me it's like the effects from a sugar rush of too many cookies at the holidays—not a good feeling. The first time I see Brent Heath smile is when he's looking at Jade. "I am pleased to inform you that the interior furnishings for this project will be as impressive as the building itself. I've worked day and night to ensure that the special needs of the older population in the Tucson Valley Retirement Community are balanced with the high quality items that only I can provide."

She pauses for dramatic effect, and I notice that everyone in the meeting is entranced, as if hanging on every word that she says. Even Tracy is leaning forward on her elbows, expectantly awaiting Jade's report. I don't get it. She's just going to talk about couches and chairs and tables. What's the big deal?

"I've brought my own technology for this technology report," she giggles. The audience in the room parrots back her laughter. She sets up a tripod with a pull-out screen. Holding a clicker, she advances images on her laptop that she projects onto the screen with a mini projector. She sets all of this up so fluidly that no one even seems bothered by the passage of a few minutes' time. "And these are the ergonomic chairs I was talking with Tracy about recently. They will be in use at every individual computer station as well as at conference tables for any group collaboration."

Brenda raises her hand.

"Yes?" asks Jade, so kindly it's like she's talking to her elderly grandmother, which Brenda does not appreciate at all.

"Not all of us need accommodations. Please tell me that this center won't look like an adult daycare." She rolls her eyes and shakes her head back and forth.

"Of course not. The accommodations are so subtle, that unless you are looking for them, you won't find them, and that's the beauty. Whatever a person needs—or doesn't need—will be there! Does that make sense?" Her delicate condescending tone amuses me but not Brenda. When Brenda doesn't respond, Jade returns to her presentation. "There will be stations throughout the center that have all of the needed ports for charging technology or connecting to other devices or to sign into virtual meetings or entertainment. No one will ever have to look for a place to plug in. Oliver and I have been in close communication about how my skills can achieve his architectural goals." She looks at Oliver and smiles. He smiles back. "And let me explain the furnishings for our virtual reality area."

I look offstage and see Mario walking down the hallway dragging another mop bucket behind him. Poor guy might as well stop. Everyone in this meeting was on the construction site today. There's going to be more dirt. Plus, the wind has picked up, and I know that Tracy fancies an open window when there's a breeze. If I were Mario, I'd clean the floors once a week and just accept the fact that nothing is going to be perfect until this project is completed, but I'm not Mario, and he's the best Director of Maintenance and Facilities in the state of Arizona.

"Rosi?"

"Huh?" I return to the meeting and realize that Mr. Heath is waiting for my answer to a question that I didn't hear.

Mr. Heath sighs. "Tracy has given you the floor to share your thoughts about the marketing for the open house. Do you have anything to contribute or would you rather continue to daydream?"

I can feel the heat rise up my neck. "Of course. Sorry. I was just...just thinking about how grateful...yes, how grateful Tracy and I are to have you all here, to know that your contributions will help to make our little retirement community the envy of the state. As far as the open house, as long as construction completes by the 27th and the furnishings are installed by the 29th, we will hold our ribbon-cutting ceremony on the 30th which will open the technology center to our residents. Local media has been contacted, but I will be sure to update them as the project progresses."

"That sounds fantastic, Rosi," says Mayor Leo. "I can't wait to show off what's being accomplished here."

I appreciate the friendly words. "Thanks, Leo."

"Okay, that's a wrap," says Mr. Heath. "I expect your team to finish this project on time," he says, addressing Jakob. "If you screw this up, you'll regret ever bidding on this contract."

Jakob frowns. "We will finish on time, *Brent.*"

"Mr. Heath," he corrects. "This meeting is adjourned." He gathers his things into his briefcase and

walks out of the room. No one dares to move until he's gone.

"He's insufferable," Jakob says to Tracy.

"I know," she says, patting Jakob's arm. "But he came highly recommended for this project. You'll never have to work with him again once our tech center is done."

"Never has a truer statement been spoken," he says.

"Your tattoos are so cool."

I turn my head to the other side of the table where Jade is pawing at Oliver's arm.

"I have a tattoo, too," she giggles, "Only you can't see it—at least not here."

Oliver smiles, amused by the aggressively flirtatious young woman who won't stop touching his arm.

"I'm looking forward to dinner tonight," I say loudly to Oliver.

He stands up and steps away from handsy Jade. "Yeah, Rosi. We'll have a blast. See you at 7:00." He pushes his chair into the table on the stage and turns to walk away.

I can't help but be amused by the look of shock on Jade's face as her mind tries to puzzle together why I'm getting a *date* with Oliver and not her, and I don't fill in the Keaton piece of the puzzle. Keep the confusion alive.

Chapter 3

"Hey, Dad. How are you?" I ask as I step outside onto my patio to call my parents before my dinner with Keats and Oliver. "Awesome. Is Mom driving you crazy yet? Ha ha. I can't wait for you to see the tech center. Yeah, it's coming along. I know. Construction projects always run late, but the construction manager is a real tyrant. I think we will stay on schedule. I'm so glad you and Mom are coming back to Arizona early this year. I know, right? Thanksgiving in Tucson Valley. Should be fun." My doorbell rings. "Hey! I have to go. Keats is here. I will. You tell Mom hello, too. Hugs to you both." I push the red button on my phone as I open the slider back into my condo.

"Come in!" I yell.

Keaton opens the door, and Barley greets him by jumping on his chest and licking his arms. "Down, girl. I'm happy to see you, too." He gently pushes Barley off and greets me with a kiss. "Why are you smiling so big?" he asks, giving me a hug.

"Am I? I suppose I'm happy to see you," I laugh. "And I just talked to Dad. He and Mom are coming to

Tucson Valley in November. They will be here by the end of Thanksgiving."

"That's exciting."

"Yeah. It really is. I didn't realize how much I missed them until I found out they were coming months earlier than usual. It will be nice having someone familiar close again."

"Hmm, *familiar?* That makes me sound like a stranger," Keaton frowns.

"I'm sorry! That's not what I mean. It's just that everything has been so new these last eight months. My parents coming back brings a part of the Midwest with them that I miss. But…" I pull Keaton by the top of his shirt until he stands before me. "There is nowhere I'd rather be than right here with you." I bop him on the nose and kiss him on the lips for as long as Barley allows until she starts barking between us. "Can you take Barley outside while I change? I need ten minutes."

"Are you sure you don't need help getting dressed?" He winks at me.

"I'm good!" I point to the sliding door. "Barley needs you, though."

Keaton hangs his head in mocked defeat as he grabs Barley's ball and takes her outside.

It's a surprisingly pleasant 79 degrees this evening. Heavenly. I choose a pair of jean capris and a red and white polka-dotted short-sleeved shirt. I pin the sides of my long hair back with a barrette on each side. I study my face in the mirror. Forty doesn't look nearly as old as I thought it would look when I was twenty. My skin is still relatively wrinkle free thanks to my diligent moisturizing routine and sunscreen application. I haven't found a stray gray hair for a few weeks now, and thanks to my job that doesn't allow me much time to sit, (and the fact that my office building is connected to the sports center), I've been able to work out a bit and stay active. When I'm satisfied with my assessment in the mirror, I call for Barley and Keaton.

Barley barrels into the condo, knocking over a vase on a side table with her tail. "Barley! Chill! For Pete's Sake!" Only she thinks I'm calling her for *treats* because she jumps up on my waist which causes me to fall backwards where I land against my inside terrarium that Keaton had given me for my birthday. "Ouch! Ouch! Stupid cactus!"

I look up at Keaton who has banished Barley to the bedroom. He has a sly grin on his face and is shaking his head back and forth. "Cactus spines? Again?" he asks.

"Again."

I sit on the couch and pull the spines from my elbow, grateful that at least this time they are tiny, while Keaton gets the antibacterial cream from my medicine cabinet in the bathroom.

"You're kind of a walking disaster," he says much more sweetly than the words themselves sound.

"Hey! Barley knocked me over. It wasn't my fault."

"I'm just grateful that I have a chance to play rescuer again."

"Oh, is that what this is?" I pull out the last spine, apply the cream, and grab my purse. "Let's go. We don't want to be late. Can you do me a favor and not mention this to Oliver?"

"Hmm. I'll consider it. What's in it for me?"

"Your life. You will maintain your life."

"Aw, that sounds serious. The secret is ours." He kisses me on the cheek and follows me out the door.

We are meeting Oliver at Casa de Comidas. He's staying at a local hotel for the night before returning to

Vegas. The restaurant is busy for a Tuesday night in October. The cooling temperatures bring more people out which is ironic considering that the 80 degrees I'd seen on my outdoor thermometer as we left my condo would be considered warming-up temperatures in the Midwest and would signal a consideration to turn on the air conditioning. It's amazing how the body adapts to the temperature changes, though, because I'm feeling so comfortable any time the temps lower to the 80s. I wonder what it will feel like when I hit my menopause days. If they are anything like my mom experienced, I'll be living with a bowl of ice cubes at the ready all day long. Let's hope those days are far away.

We take a table in the back of the restaurant and order a pitcher of margaritas while we wait for Oliver to arrive. "So, what did you think of Oliver Putnam when you met him today?" Keaton asks.

He stretches his arms over his head, and the ripples of muscles on his arms mesmerize me. "Huh?"

"What did you think of Oliver?" he repeats.

"He seems confident. Nice, though. He seems on top of things regarding the project."

"Hey, man!" Oliver says, walking toward our table. He's changed into khaki pants and a green polo shirt that accentuates his tattoos, though I can't make out what they are supposed to be, maybe some sort of abstract art? "Sorry I'm late!"

Keaton stands up to embrace his old college buddy with a giant bear hug. "So good to see you." He pats Oliver on the back before releasing him.

"Awesome to see you again, too. It's been too long. What, like four or five years?"

"Something like that," Keaton says.

"Good to see you again, too, Rosi," Oliver says, giving me a much gentler hug.

"Who would have thought that I'd get a reunion with my college buddy because he's working in my town with my girlfriend?" Keaton says as he shakes his head in disbelief. "I'm a lucky guy."

"I know. Fate works like that. Remember how we met in the first place?" Oliver laughs so loudly and deeply that the people at the next table stop to stare.

"Dang straight I do. You nearly took me out on your scooter. I could have throttled you I was so mad!"

Oliver laughs again. I'm taking it all in, the two grown men caught up in memories from the past, oblivious to anyone else in the room but the two of them. The waiter refocuses the conversation as we are delivered a basket of chips and salsa and place our order for a second pitcher of margaritas.

"So, Rosi, tell me how you met this goofball," Oliver says, dipping his chip into the spicy salsa bowl.

"I was taking a walk while he was landscaping, and let's just say I kept *falling* into his path," I giggle. "Plus, I have a cute puppy. Puppies help most relationships."

"Gotcha. Fair point, though I thought Keats was a cat guy."

Keaton holds up his hand. "I am an equal pet lover. No judgment zone when it comes to four-legged critters. Your turn for the interrogation, Ollie. How'd you get brought onto the Tucson Valley Tech Center project?"

"Vegas is really becoming a technology hub with lots of tech startups and bigger companies coming to the area. A few years ago, my company decided to pivot from the residential architecture market to the tech market, and we've been designing tech centers ever since."

"Been pretty lucrative?" Keaton asks with a giant grin on his face. He takes a long drink of his margarita.

"You could say that."

"Now all you need is to find your señorita like I have," says Keaton.

"Me? Naw, I'm playing the field, and that's all fine by me. I've done the relationship thing. Those days are a thing of the past."

"How are the kids?"

"They're great. I get them every other week. Can't complain." Oliver turns to me and smiles. "What about you two?"

"What do you mean?" I take a drink, too, suddenly feeling my stomach getting queasy and recalling that I'd been too busy to eat lunch.

"Kids in your future?"

I spit out my drink, sending tequila flying out of my mouth and landing on Keaton's cheek. "Oops! Sorry. No more kids in my future. I have a grown son."

Keaton wipes off his cheek and winks at me, reminding me that I'm enough—that I'm all he wants in his life. We've had this talk before. "Tell us more about the Tucson Valley project," he says, redirecting the conversation from sensitive topics.

"It's a medium-size project for our company as far as size and scope, but as far as potential for future work, it's huge. The Roland Price Technology Center will be groundbreaking for senior center and retirement communities around the country. It's the kind of place that people will try to emulate. It will be *the* place that others will want in their communities. And we will be the first architect to field those calls because of our designs here."

"That's so exciting, Oliver. I had no idea that our project would be so innovative. I still can't believe that Tracy's idea is this popular."

"It's not just Tracy," says Keaton. "It was Mr. Price and his experience in the tech industry as well as his love for Tucson Valley that planted the seed in Tracy's mind and helped it to grow."

"Certainly." I flutter my eyes to refocus on Keaton as my vision gets wonky. "What do you think about Brent…hiccup…Heath…hiccup?" Keaton hands me a chip.

"He's a jerk."

"Oh, well, yeah, I…hiccup…agree." I take a slow drink.

"Seriously, the guy has real narcissist tendencies. He acts like he's keeping the project focused on a tight timeline, but he's the one driving Jakob's workers away by his rudeness and temper. If this project runs late, it's because Brent Heath's temper drove them away, not because Jakob or anyone else screwed up."

"Yeah, Jakob is getting the…hiccup…brunt of his wrath. I've…hiccup…witnessed it many times. Except with Jade. She's the only one he's nice…hiccup…to."

"Why's that?" Keaton asks.

"Have you seen this woman?" Oliver laughs.

"Disgusting pig," Keaton says, punching Oliver in the arm.

"Why do you think I'm still single?" He throws up his hands in acceptance of his flaws.

"I…I…hiccup…oh no!" I throw my hand over my mouth where I've just thrown up salsa and chips. I grab a napkin, turn my head, and spit them out. I excuse myself and run to the bathroom where I make the toilet just in time for the rest of my chips and salsa to make their less than graceful exit from my mouth.

When I return to the table, a plate of enchiladas verdes sits next to my empty margarita glass. I put my hand over my mouth again, my eyes starting to water.

"Rosi, let me take you home. You don't look too good. No offense," says Keaton as he rubs my back.

"I'm really sorry. I haven't eaten much today, and the margarita and the stress and…"

Oliver grabs my hand from across the table. "Go home, Rosi. It's okay. I'll be back in Tucson Valley before the project is complete. We can go out again."

"I'm really sorry. Keaton was so looking forward to this dinner," I wipe away a stray tear. "Wait! I'll walk home. It's only a half mile back to my place."

"Are you crazy? I'm not going to let you walk home."

"You can't stop me, either. Please, Keaton. The fresh air will feel so good. The senior center is right over there," I say, pointing to my workplace. "That was one of the perks of buying the condo that I did. It's a super short walk from work to home. Watch me walk to the senior center. I'll use my key to get into the building and walk through the hallways to the back of the building. Then it's literally one block away."

"I don't like this idea, Rosi."

"I am a forty-year-old woman, Alex P. Keaton, and the Golden Girls are my namesake. I think I can handle a half mile walk alone. Plus, Tucson Valley has like zero crime! Why do you think Officer Daniel drives around town all day? He's just wishing for a crime to be committed on his watch."

"There is *some* crime in Tucson Valley," he says, raising his eyebrows as if I need a reminder about the murders of Salem Mansfield and Sherman Padowski.

"True, but those were very specific cases with personal connections between the victim and the murderer. No matter how much Brenda or Jan detest me, I don't think they'd try to kill me, and they are the only grumps with a grudge against me in Tucson Valley that I know of." I put my hand on Keaton's arm. "Put your phone on the table. I'll call and keep you on the line while I walk. Have a great time." I go in for a kiss, but Keaton turns his head to the side. "Oh, yeah. Good call. Sorry." I turn back to Oliver. "Take care that this guy stops drinking so I don't have to worry about *him* getting home safely."

"Will do, Rosi. I hope you feel better soon."

"Thanks!"

After a final hug and a kiss on the top of my head from Keaton, I enter his number on my phone and walk across the parking lot toward the senior center. I know that Keats is watching me the whole way. I've never had someone who loves me as much as Keaton does. We haven't used the *love* word very much because it scares us both with our history of divorces, but if the way Keaton cares for me isn't love, then I don't know what love is.

I pull out my senior center key and swipe the keypad. The building is empty except for anyone who might be using the 24-hour gym in the adjoining sports center, but as the lights go out when no one has been in the hallway for a few minutes, it looks like no one is here because I can tell through the windows that the area is dark.

"Rosi? Everything okay?"

"Everything's fine," I say into my phone. "The hall lights just kicked on, and I'm winding my way through to the back. My condo is only a block or so beyond that. How was your burrito?"

"Muy bien," he says.

"Great. Now, go back to Oliver."

"Okay, but don't hang up."

"I won't."

Sometimes when I pass the auditorium, I think about Sherman Padowski's death. I didn't think about it today when we had our meeting on the stage, but I do now when it's late in the evening and no one else is in the building. I walk a little faster to get out of the building, reaching the back door that will become the main entrance onto the sidewalk that will lead to the Roland Price Technology Center. I open the door, checking that it closes firmly behind me.

Then I'm faced with a choice. Go around the construction site, adding another couple of minutes to my walk home or walk through the construction site to save time. My stomach is still rolling around, so I really want to get home. But I also remember the western diamondback rattlesnake skin that Gabby had shown me today. Reminding myself that rattlesnakes aren't confined to property lines, I decide to cut through the construction site. I turn on the flashlight on my phone though the lights from the outside of the senior center are pretty bright, bright enough to keep me from tripping over a wheelbarrow or misplaced ladder.

The technology center is mammoth in size. At three stories high, it's the tallest building in the Tucson Valley Retirement Community. The yellow-painted concrete, something Tracy and I had fought for, lights up under the Arizona night sky. With Keaton's brightly colored landscape choices (because I know he's getting that contract), this place is not only going to be amazing on the inside but gorgeous on the outside. Only a few more weeks, and Jade's furnishings will be delivered and assembled. The electrical work will be complete. Carpets and tiling done. I can't wait. And the fact that we've been able to complete nearly the impossible by going from land to design to a complete and functional building within only a few short months is nothing short of astonishing, especially with a crew of revolving people. I'm thinking about Jakob's efficiency when I see something out of the corner of my eye and just out of the spotlight of my phone. I pivot my phone ahead of me by a few feet and to the right. Yes, there. Something is leaning against the outside door of the tech center—something that looks out of place. I raise my cellphone so that the light is shining directly at the front door. "Oh nooooooooo!"

"Rosi? Rosi? *ROSI? WHAT'S WRONG?*"

I can hear Keaton's concerned voice yelling at me through the phone, but I can't answer yet. I put my hand over my heart to steady my breathing and take a step forward to confirm my worst fears. I check for a pulse, something I've perfected with too much practice since my arrival in Tucson Valley. Only then do I respond to Keaton's frantic questions. "I'm okay."

"Thank the Lord. What's going on? Did you see that snake?"

"Nope. No snake. But I need you and Oliver to come to the construction site right away."

"Why? Rosi, what's going on?"

"Brent Heath is here."

"Okay, the construction manager? Working late? Is he being a jerk? Oliver's been telling me about him."

"No, he's…he's not being a jerk."

"What is it, Rosi?"

"He's dead."

Chapter 4

Keaton and Oliver arrive on the scene at the same time that Officer Dan Daniel is walking toward me. I believe I've caught Officer Daniel by surprise as the shirt of his police uniform hangs untucked around his waist, his nametag askew. "Rosi, are you okay?" His first question is very much appreciated. Our relationship has evolved nicely since the first time I stumbled upon a dead body in Tucson Valley, and though his policing abilities are best described as lackluster, his heart for this community makes up for any shortcomings.

Keaton reaches for my hand and pulls me in for a hug before I can answer Officer Daniel. "I was so worried about you. I should never have let you walk home alone. I am so stupid."

"Walk home from where?" asks Officer Daniel.

"Oh, dang," says Oliver, shining his cellphone light on Brent Heath's body that is in a seated position leaning up against the front door of the technology center.

"I was having dinner at Casa de Comidas with Keats and Oliver." I point to Oliver who waves his hand at Officer Daniel. "They are friends from college, and Oliver is the lead architect for the new tech center. My stomach has been a little upset tonight, so I wanted to walk home."

Officer Daniel looks at Keaton and shakes his head back and forth. "Shame, shame, shame," he says judgmentally.

Keaton bites the inside of his cheek. I can tell because his face sucks in. He's going to beat himself up over this for a long time though I don't think I was in any real danger. Or was I? I shudder involuntarily at the thought that whoever did this to Brent Heath is watching us all right now.

"I took a shortcut through the senior center and decided to walk through the construction site."

"That was dumb," Officer Daniel says as he surveys the site. "You could have tripped yourself up on any of this stuff. There are tools and supplies and wires and piping everywhere, Rosi."

"I know. I really wanted to be home, so I took this route." I put my hand over my stomach to remind him of my pressing predicament. And it reminds *me* that I still don't feel well. I take a step away from the group to pass gas. They just think I need a minute to myself. It happens. Why fight it?

"Are those nails?" I hear Keaton ask as the three men stare at Brent Heath's body.

"Sure looks like it," says Officer Daniel. "Right through the heart. Not a fun way to go."

"That's an understatement," says Keaton.

"I don't see any nail gun," Oliver says, looking through items on the ground next to Brent's body.

"Don't touch anything!" yells Officer Daniel. "I'll call in backup. This is a crime scene now."

"The whole site is a crime scene?" I ask, returning to the group as I hold my stomach tightly.

"Yes, Rosi. Who knows what evidence is out here in this mess?" says Officer Daniel.

"But, Dan! That will put this project behind schedule, and that will cost money. We are contracted to pay laborers until the project is complete, and if they can't work because the site is shut down, we will still owe them! And there is equipment that's been rented that will require extensions, and everything is so perfectly choreographed to work together. If electric is delayed, then the floors are delayed. Then the furnishings are delayed, and then…"

"I'm sorry, Rosi, that a man has been murdered on your construction site, but that's just the way it is. Now tell me about this guy. Do you know him?"

Oliver answers for me, and I appreciate the reprieve from the mental gymnastics of anxieties that are flipping through my mind. "Brent Heath is the man's name. He is the construction manager for this project."

"I thought some guy named Jakob was in charge. I've met him out here before when I stopped by to check on the progress."

"Jakob Beacher is the general contractor, the day-to-day supervisor. Brent Heath oversaw the entire project, but more from a financial perspective. He's the guy that worked with Tracy Lake and the board to ensure that what they want to happen with this project is clearly outlined. Jakob's job was to implement this plan with his laborers."

"Do they work for the same company?"

"No," I say. "Both were chosen through a bidding process. Jakob is from the Phoenix area. Brent is from—was from—Nogales."

"Is it normal for there to be people on the construction site after dark?"

"Not at all, Dan. There is nothing normal about this. Can't you remove the body and let the work continue?"

Officer Daniel looks at me like I'm crazy. "Now that I know how intimately the victim was associated with this location, that's even more reason to shut it down for investigation. I'm sorry, Rosi. It has to be done. Is there anything else you can think of to add tonight before I let you go?"

"Like what? Oops. Excuse me," I say, as I burp loudly.

"Rosi needs to get home, Dan. Can we go now?" Keaton puts a protective arm around my shoulders.

"Fine. Call me in the morning."

Officer Xena Whitley arrives on the scene, replaced by Officer Emma Prince who didn't last more than six weeks after getting put on disciplinary leave for giving a petty thief a ride home after robbing the local bakery. She'd said she felt sorry for the guy and that he'd only wanted a banana cream pie really badly that day. I can't understand why anyone would *ever* want a banana cream pie. Officer Xena Whitley is a competitive weightlifter who stands at least half a foot taller than Officer Daniel, though her voice is higher than mine. She puts off a very strong *don't mess with me* vibe with her tight jet-black, slicked-back bun. I hope that she can help Dan solve this case quickly so that we can get back to work.

"Hello, Officer Whitley." She waves. "I'll call Tracy and Jakob," I say.

"Good. Tell them to expect calls from me as well. And we'll need to see the security cameras." He raises his eyebrows in judgment. "Please tell me there are security cameras here and that they are turned on."

I recall a very similar conversation after the murder of Sherman Padowski when the security cameras had been turned off. "I'll check first thing tomorrow morning."

"Good. Go tend to that stomach," he says. "You're not fooling anyone."

"Oh, uh, sorry," I say, mortified that my stepping-away ruse had failed. I walk quickly toward the sidewalk that will take me back to my condo so that no one can see my glowing face.

"Rosi! Wait! Let me drive you," yells Keaton.

"Nope! Nope! I'm good. I'm good!" I walk quicker, feeling the rush of my stomach start to shake free the blockage in my gut. I don't even stop walking when I trip over a paint can. I stumble but keep walking. It's not until I've exited my bathroom twenty minutes later that I realize I've created a pattern of yellow footprints down my hallway.

My prince of a boyfriend stands with his arms outstretched where I collapse against his chest and cry out my frustrations.

Chapter 5

My conversation with Tracy last night had not gone well. She'd been beside herself as was I about the delays Brent Heath's death might cause with the completion of the technology center. So many things have been planned and scheduled and pieced together like an elaborate puzzle, that shutting things down is going to mess everything up. She's not wrong. Not wrong at all. It's funny how neither of us bemoaned the loss of Brent Heath, just the inconvenience his death investigation was going to have on our lives. I feel a bit guilty about that. He was a bully and a tyrant, but he was still a human being.

Jakob Beacher's phone conversation with me had gone much better from Brent's perspective should he be watching from above. Jakob is a much more emotional man than he'd let on. We'd agreed to meet with the team again this morning as Jade and Oliver are still in town. Only this time the whole HOA board is coming, too, which means Jan and Brenda and Bob and Leo and a couple of other members without big, annoying personalities that I don't know well. I really wish that Jan and Frank had stayed in Illinois a little longer. Having to see Jan in Phoenix at our convention had been enough *Jan time* for me. Jan and

Brenda together are more than twice the amount of aggravation. Their ability to irritate multiplies exponentially when they are together.

Barley jumps on the bed after being let out to pee by Keaton. He spent the night "just to make sure I was okay," he'd said. I appreciated the company, and Barley has someone else to annoy in bed besides me. She has a way of finding the most comfortable sleeping position near my head, on my head, over my face. She licks me across the forehead followed by a kiss from Keaton on the cheek. "Your tummy feeling better?"

"Yeah, sorry about that. I feel good now. It was the perfect storm of an empty stomach mixed with a margarita pitcher and spicy salsa and stress."

"Irritable bowel syndrome?"

"Ha, ha! Yep, that's the diagnosis—at least my semi-professional, self-diagnosis." I throw my arms open wide. "What's not to love about me now?" I roll over onto my side laughing. Barley joins the party by jumping back and forth over my legs and barking. Keaton adds himself to the melee and plops on the bed, snuggling up to me until we are spooning, only Barley wedges herself between the two of us, rotating 360 degrees two times before settling half on the bed and half on my butt.

Keaton leans over Barley's head and whispers so quietly I can barely make out what he's saying. "I love everything about you, Rosisophia Doroche Laruee. Everything. Sour stomach and all."

I don't answer, choosing to close my eyes for a moment and to place this memory away in a safe place in my brain.

"Good morning, Mario," I say as I pass him in the hallway on the way to my office.

"Hey, Rosi. Rough night?" he asks, patting me on the arm.

"Word spreads fast."

"Tracy asked me to set the stage up for a big meeting. I'm pretty sure that everyone in Tucson Valley and beyond will know before lunch. Celia actually told me before Tracy because she heard from Karen who heard from Jan who heard from Brenda about what happened."

"What? Celia's running with the gaggle of gossips now? I thought she was better than that."

"Oh, she is. Those women simply amuse her, though Karen's different. She and Celia have gone out for lunch a couple of times."

"Yes, Karen is different—different in the best way possible."

"Oh, Rosi! There you are," says Tracy, wrapping her arms around me and pulling me close. "Why oh why must you always be the one to discover the body? Tsk. Tsk. It's the thing of nightmares."

"Well, technically, Brenda discovered the body the night of the '60s Send-off Concert."

"That wretched woman is going to be in a mood today for sure. First, she loses the mayoral election to Leo Lestman and now George has left her."

"What?"

"You hadn't heard the news?"

"I don't travel in the same circles as you," I say, smiling.

"Don't you dare group me in with those women, Rosi Laruee! Oh, sorry, I know your mom—"

"No offense taken. I am positive I would have heard the news had my mom been in Tucson Valley. Who told you?"

"Safia called this morning. She was quite animated. She kept saying *poodles, this is so exciting!*"

"Yikes. I don't like Brenda any more than the next person, but to call the breakup of her marriage *exciting* goes a bit far."

"Brenda is not very nice to Safia, not nice at all."

"Fair point. And I guess someone wasn't very nice to Brent Heath, either."

"Is it true that he was killed with a nail gun?" Tracy shudders and squeezes her eyes shut as if trying to block out what she is imagining. I wish I could only imagine the scene instead of recollecting it over and over in my mind.

"Unfortunately, every bit of that story I told you is the truth." I look at my watch. "We'd better go. The meeting starts in a few minutes."

"Ugh. Somehow the board is going to twist this situation into being my fault. It will be *my fault* that this project is going to be overbudget."

"I won't let that happen, boss. Come on." I link my arm through Tracy's as we walk to the auditorium for the second meeting in the last twenty-four hours.

Jakob Beacher stands at the head of the table talking with Officer Daniel who has invited himself to the meeting. I suppose it's appropriate as everyone he wants to talk to is here in the same place. Jakob's eyes are red, not like red from crying, but red from exhaustion. He sounded like I'd woken him when I'd called late last night. I imagine he never went back to sleep.

Oliver and Jade walk into the meeting together, talking jovially as if they'd known each other for years. Maybe they have. Maybe they've worked together on other projects. When they see that Tracy and I are staring at them, they stop talking and separate to opposite sides of the table.

"Hey, Rosi." Oliver plants a kiss on my cheek. "How are you doing this morning?"

"Never been better."

He smiles. "Yeah, kind of a dumb question. Just think, though. It can only improve from here."

"You really don't know me very well. I'm on quite a streak."

He looks like he's about to question what I mean when Brenda and Jan enter the room followed by Bob, Leo, and two men that I don't know other than by appearance: one of them tall and thin with a fully bald head who walks with a cane, and the other, a foot shorter and slightly plump with a full head of black hair (perhaps a toupee?) who walks with a limp.

"Thank you all for coming back today, and welcome to our new guests. It is with a heavy heart that I have to confirm the passing of our construction manager, Mr. Brent Heath. He was kille…"

Officer Daniel waves his arms wildly at Jakob. "That's enough, Mr. Beacher. No need to spill all of the details. Thank you. Ladies and gentlemen, I am Officer Dan Daniel, the police chief for Tucson Valley."

His introduction is amusing as literally everyone in the room has met Officer Daniel, most many, many times except for Jade who seems disinterested as she files her nails, her artificial eyelashes blocking my view of whether she's paying attention to Dan through her peripheral vision or not.

"I'd like to ask a few questions of the group before you begin, and if you don't mind, I'll sit quietly and observe the rest of the meeting, you know, for police business."

"Of course," Jakob says, stroking his goatee and adjusting his reading glasses as if he doesn't know what to do with his nervous energy.

"When was the last time you each saw Mr. Heath? I'll start with you, Ms.—" he says, looking at Jade.

"Jade," she says.

"Thank you, Ms. Jade. What is your role—"

"No, just Jade. My name is Jade."

"Oh," Officer Daniel wrinkles his nose. "Uh, Just Jade, what position do you hold in this project?"

I have to stifle a laugh behind my hand.

"I am the interior designer for the Roland Price Technology Center. I chose the furnishings, the carpeting, tile, paint colors, things like that—with Ms. Lake's input, naturally." She smiles sweetly at Tracy who returns her smile.

"And the last time you saw Mr. Heath?"

"I last saw Brent yesterday—here—at this same table in this same room."

"And you didn't see him after the meeting?"

She pauses before answering, brushing her blonde hair with her fingers. It's very seductive the way she untangles her locks, slowing weaving her fingers in and around her hair, and I wonder if it's a ploy to fluster Officer Daniel because it will probably work. "Brent made an attempt to see me, but I had better things to do."

"Meaning?" asks Officer Daniel.

"Maybe we can discuss this in private—after the meeting?" She gives him a small smile, and I can tell we are losing him quickly to the spell of a pretty woman.

"Yes, yes, that can be arranged." He clears his throat several times, flustered by Jade's request for alone time—because that's how he will see it.

Dan, Dan, Dan. I shake my head back and forth, disappointed in his stereotypical follies. Needing to rescue him from himself, I pipe in with my answer to the original question. "Officer Daniel, I saw Brent leave the meeting yesterday and walk toward the construction site. From my office window, which partially looks out over the site, I saw him talking to Gabby and a few of the other construction workers. That's the last time I saw him until, uh, last night."

"Good. Thank you, Rosi. And this Gabby and the other workers in the site? Might I get a list of their names?" he asks, turning his attention back to Jakob.

"Yes. I can do that. They were all quite alarmed about the news. They want to finish their jobs, get this project completed *on time*," he enunciates as he looks at the board members. Tracy nods her head enthusiastically next to me.

"Well, that is not going to happen until we have finished our investigation here."

"It *has* to happen, Officer Daniel," says Jan. "If Ms. Lake can't get this project completed on time, then it will cost the retirement community more money than we have budgeted for this project." She pauses before continuing. "And we might need to find a new director of the Tucson Valley Senior Center who can carry out our vision."

"Hold up," I say, finding the need to stand up for extra emphasis. "Tracy Lake has more heart for the Tucson Valley Retirement Community than anyone else here. You are acting as if it was *her* fault that Brent Heath was murdered on our property."

"Perhaps," Jan says, taking a slow, deep breath. "Perhaps if she'd chosen a different crew, no one would have felt the need to off the boss!" She crosses her arms triumphantly as if she's delivered the final zinger that will seal Tracy's fate.

"Wait a second." The realization of why Jan is coming down so hard on Tracy reaches its destination in my brain. "This is about Allen, isn't it?"

"What are you talking about, Rosi?" Jan turns her head away from me.

I can feel all eyes on the two of us, nobody wanting to interrupt. "You want your nephew to take over Tracy's job."

"Nonsense!"

"Leave Jan alone. Quit being a bully," says Brenda, only she doesn't speak with her usual intensity. Upon examination, Brenda looks a mess. Her eyes are red, and her makeup is smudged. I make a mental note to tell Mom though I feel a flutter of empathy pass through my heart, remembering what it's like when your husband leaves you.

"Ladies, we have more important matters to tend to than timelines. I am trying to conduct a murder investigation." Officer Daniel opens his eyes wide and looks between Jan, Brenda, and me, daring one of us to speak. "Good. Let's carry on. Oliver, tell me the last time you saw Mr. Heath."

Oliver frowns as if whatever he is remembering is not pleasant. Even while frowning, he's got an irresistible look about him, but kind of like when Wesley charmed me way back in high school. I learned a long time ago not to get too sucked in by good looks and charm alone. "Brent and I had a *discussion* after the meeting."

"About what?"

"He didn't like my design choices for the virtual reality wing of the building."

"Go on."

"Specifically, he didn't like that my designs called for a rounded structure to be attached to the back of the building. He was a big fan of symmetry and wanted me to redo my design to make that part of the building flow with ninety degree walls. I argued for my design, reminding him that the purpose of this building was to be a beacon for technological innovation for senior centers. That includes the inside *and* outside as far as I'm concerned. My plans were approved by Ms. Lake and the board here." He pauses to make eye contact with all of the board members. "I wouldn't give in, and he didn't like that."

"How did your conversation end?"

"Let's just say he was less than happy with my decision to carry out my plan—our team plan. He said something like *we'll see about that* and stormed off."

"Did you take that as a threat to your plans?"

"I don't feel threatened, Officer Daniel. Little intimidates me." He looks at Officer Daniel until the poor man has to look away for fear that Oliver's eyes will bore a hole through him.

"Can we please get to the meeting agenda?" asks the lanky, tall man with the bald head.

"Okay, Pete. I think I am done here anyway. Does anyone else have anything they'd like to add about your experiences with Mr. Heath?"

No one says a word, so Jakob uses that as his cue to speak. "Officer Daniel, can you please tell us when we might be able to get back to work? This project is on a fine timeline with opening set for late October. Is that still feasible?"

"That's only a few weeks away."

"Thank you, Captain Calendar," says Brenda sarcastically.

"Officer Whitley and I, along with a forensic team from Phoenix, will be combing the site for clues today. In fact, they are already out there working now. I can't make any promises. And, please, if you think of anything, give me a call. Stay out of that site. No one enter. Ms. Lake, those security tapes I asked about?"

"Oh, yes. I pulled them this morning right away. I'm afraid I have some bad news."

Officer Daniel grunts his frustration. "Don't you dare tell me that the cameras were shut off."

"They were on," Tracy says softly.

"Good. That's very good news."

"But not the whole time."

"Excuse me?" Officer Daniel asks.

"What?"

"Huh?"

"Why?"

A chorus of questions float around the room.

"I don't know. There is video footage of the whole day and the day before. The video keeps the feed for two days or longer if we wanted to program the setting for a different length. But, the video from yesterday stops at 6:00 p.m. Someone shut off the security feed."

"Who has that kind of access?" asks Bob who has been quiet for the entire meeting.

"Well, I do, of course. And Rosi and Mario. We are the only ones who know where the security system is located and how to operate it."

Officer Daniel gives me the stink eye, a look I'd known well from my mom that embodies a look of judgment accusing me of hiding something. "Look! There have been a lot of people in and out of this building for weeks. The security system was set up in a small closet near the back door. It wasn't locked. Anyone could have been in that room."

"What about a security camera that monitors the hallway outside the room with the security system—so you could see who was going into the room?" asks Jade, picking something off her black blazer.

"Excellent question," Officer Daniel says, straightening his shoulders as if he were even remotely in Jade's league. He is so easily charmed by the opposite sex.

"We moved the backdoor camera to the construction site," says Tracy. "Trying to save money," she offers, as if that little bit of information will please the board, but none of them are smiling.

"Look, Dan, you are taking entirely too much of our time. Can't you talk to people later today?" Brenda asks, every ounce of her polished face screaming as much frustration as possible.

"Please write your names and numbers on this paper," Officer Daniel says as he pulls a simple scratch piece of paper out of his front pocket, not a single notepad in sight. What kind of police officer doesn't carry a notepad?

"Jakob, can we turn our attention back to the construction project? With Brent, uh, out of the picture, so to speak, can we trust that you can carry on the construction managerial responsibilities?" asks Mayor Leo.

"Of course I can." Jakob looks at the pairs of eyes that range from varying degrees of trust to doubt. "I absolutely can," he reiterates. "As soon as we get the green light to proceed, we will. Oliver gave a fine report yesterday about the concrete. The electrician is ready to go which will be followed by Jade's overseeing of the flooring and interior painting and furnishings. The only hiccup is the virtual reality room because of it's unique round feature. That is the only structural part of the building that is not complete. It's more complicated but can be completed as designed." He nods at Oliver as acknowledgement of his winning that argument in design over Brent.

"What kind of financial burden is this delay putting on our project?" asks Jan, grimacing at Tracy as if it's her fault that Brent Heath was murdered a few feet from her office.

"We are contracted to pay our workers through the 30th—whether they work or not."

"That's absurd," says Brenda. "Who agreed to something so dumb?"

"You did," I say. "It was a contractual offering that Jakob's company proposed. They agreed to a lower pay rate—but a daily pay rate even if work is slowed—to get the job done by the 30th, but for any day past the 30th, they get overtime for every hour worked."

"That gives them incentive to be lazy on the job!" she says, throwing her pen across the table.

"I take offense to that, lady! My reputation precedes me. I manage a hard-working team. The faster they get their projects done, the sooner we can move on to another project, and we get more yearly projects because of our quality of work and our timeliness. This delay only hurts us because we will be late on other projects we have lined up at the end of the year. Don't you dare accuse me…"

"Stop! Bob stands up and slams his hand on the table so hard that the stage floor vibrates. "We are forgetting the purpose of this project. And a man has lost his life for goodness' sake! We should be pulling together, supporting the police, and tightening up the completion plan for when the project can reopen. Jakob, you have our full confidence. *Our full confidence.* Until then, do what you need to do. Meet with Jade and Oliver and your construction crew. Officer Daniel, talk to whomever you need to talk to. Scour the site for clues. The rest of us should stay out of it and let the professionals work. Is that clear?"

No one answers. The point is taken. The meeting is over.

"Thank you, Bob," says Tracy quietly. "Feel free to stay as long as you'd like, Jakob, Oliver, and Jade. The rest of us will get out of your hair. I'll be in my office if you need me." She smiles confidently, reasserting her control, bolstered by Bob's speech.

Officer Daniel follows me back to my office. He sits down across from me though he is not invited to do so. "So, what do you think, Rosi?"

"About what?"

"Who had it in for Brent Heath?"

I sigh. "I don't know, Dan. He was a jerk. He treated Jakob like a second-class citizen as well as his crew. But I don't know anyone that would hate him enough to shoot a nail gun into his chest."

"Well, I'm taking the video from the last couple of days back to the station to see if I can spot anything out of order. Can you come watch it with me later?"

"Me?"

"Yeah, you know the players. I don't."

I look at the clock. "Sure, I'll come by after lunch."

Officer Daniel gets up slowly, pausing to look at a picture of Barley on the wall. "Maybe I should get a dog," he says quietly. And then he leaves.

Chapter 6

"I'll be back late this afternoon," I holler into Tracy's office as I leave the senior center for lunch and my meeting with Officer Daniel. I'm drawn to the back door, hoping for a fresh look at the construction site in the daylight, trying to make sense of what has happened there. I see my work boots sitting on the mat by the door, waiting to be put on, waiting to walk into the construction site and oversee the changes brought by each day. But not today. Today they sit alone. Alone. Odd. Where are Tracy's work boots?

I walk out the back door and stand between the building and the police tape that has been strung about the site. A forensics team from the state is walking around the site along with Officer Daniel and Officer Whitley. They are collecting items into bags and plastic containers though I can't imagine what evidence they are gathering that could help them figure out who murdered Brent Heath with a nail gun. The site looks completely the same as it did yesterday except for the different cast of characters.

"Man, am I glad to see you." I hold on tightly to Keaton as we meet at Tuttle Park for lunch. The pickleball courts are full, the incessant pop-pop-pop of balls being hit by paddles. I'd swung by the house to grab Barley. She needs a break as much as me. Barley jumps up on Keaton, breaking up our hug. "I really need to get her into puppy school before it's too late."

"I saw a posting on the park announcement board. The enrollment date for that school Bob was telling you about starts soon. Better check it out on your way back to the car."

"Okay," I rub Barley on the belly as she's rolling on her back in the grass. She's not the only one who loves these cooler temperatures.

"How was the meeting?" Keaton takes out his cooler bag, handing me a ham and cheese sandwich and an apple along with a chocolate brownie and bottled iced tea.

"Thanks. Officer Daniel dominated most of it. No one knows anything. The security camera had been shut off at 6:00 last night. And the project is on hold until the police are done combing the construction site for clues. I'm supposed to meet Dan this afternoon to go over the video from earlier yesterday and possibly the day before; I'm really not sure."

"Do you think you'll learn anything?"

"I have no idea. Can we talk about something else? I'm getting kind of tired of murder."

Keaton laughs and hands me his brownie. "Sure thing, Rosisophia Doroche. Take my brownie, too. You might need a pick-me-up snack later today."

"Oliver is meeting with Jade," I say as I take a bite of my apple.

"The interior designer?"

"Yeah. They seemed a little chummy when then came into the meeting today."

"Oliver's a big flirt—always has been."

"Maybe. Anyway, how's work?"

"Good, although I was hoping the board would have voted on the landscaping contract by now. I need to put some orders in if I'm landscaping around the tech center."

"Sorry. I'm trying to stay out of it—conflict of interest."

"I get it."

"Barley, no!" I grab hold of Barley's leash before she goes running after a pickleball that has landed near us outside of the fence. "This dog," I say, shaking my head back and forth. "Do you want me to ask Tracy about the landscaping—on the side, of course—not at an official meeting?"

"Let's not talk about my work anymore, either," Keaton says, as he takes a long swig of tea.

"Okay. What shall we talk about?" I smile, which is always easy to do around Keaton.

"I was thinking we could make out instead of talking."

"Here?" I say, looking around the crowded park.

Keaton shrugs his shoulders as he leans against a tree. Barley snores nearby. I take another drink of my tea. Then I pull Keaton by his work shirt until we cannot get any closer with our clothes on. He kisses me first, but I kiss back seriously, letting the worry and anxiety of my day fall away. We are caught up in the moment like two teenagers in the backseat of a car on a hot date.

"Rosi? *Rosi?*"

Barley wakes up and barks at the person who repeats my name. *Repeats my name.* Oh my goodness! I whip my face away from Keaton's face so quickly that I hit the back of my head on the legs of the person standing behind me. "Ouch!"

"Rosi, what are you doing?" asks Safia. "You're in a public park. Oh, poodles, dear, you could be arrested for such a public display of affection." She giggles followed by a hiccup. "Oops!"

"I am so sorry, Safia. We were only kissing, but you are right." I look around, horrified by my lack of decorum, though no one pays us any notice but Safia.

"Hey, Safia," says Keaton, waving. "Nice to see you again."

"You, too, loverboy." The smile on Safia's face is as wide as her skirt is long.

"What brings you here on this lovely afternoon?" Keaton asks.

"I'm showing a house on the other side of the park." She points to a small brown adobe home that looks like every other home in the Tucson Valley Retirement Community, exactly like the one my parents rent every winter. "I was taking a little walk in this lovely weather. I didn't expect it to be so *hot* out here. Ha! Ha! I crack myself up, don't I?"

"Uh, well, I need to get to the police station. I have a meeting with Officer Daniel."

"Is this about that dreadful murder? Tsk. Tsk. Tsk. Not again, you poor, poor, thing."

"Good luck with your house showing, Safia. Nice to see you again."

"Toodles, poodles, Rosi! And goodbye, Keaton!" she laughs out loud to herself as she walks down the sidewalk.

I check my watch. "I need to go, Keats. Thanks for taking my mind off, uh, things."

"It was fun, Rosi," he says, kissing me on the cheek. "Maybe we could do this again sometime," he grins goofily.

"Behind closed doors. I'll call you later!" I grab Barley by the collar, and head toward my car, stopping only to snap a picture of the notice on the park announcement board about the puppy training classes.

Chapter 7

After dropping Barley off at home, I drive to the Tucson Valley Police Station. Officer Whitley sits at the front desk when I arrive. She wears a scowl on her face that matches the wavy barrette against her sleek black hair. "Hello, Officer Whitley. I'm meeting with Officer Daniel this afternoon." She points to Officer Daniel's office without a word.

I knock on Dan's door. He waves me in. "Have a seat, Rosi. I'm glad you're here. I have the video feed running onto that monitor." He points to a large computer screen hooked up to his laptop. The video is paused on the construction site with a time stamp of 8:21 a.m.

"Great. Have you watched any yet?" I pull out a water bottle and set it on the desk.

"Why would I do that?"

"Uh, because you might be anxious for leads," I say dryly.

Officer Daniel shakes his head back and forth as if he's incredulous that I'd even suggested that he'd begun to watch the surveillance footage without me. "Rosi, come here." He gestures for me to come closer. "I may have a new partner in the office, but after my experiences with

Officer Kelly and Officer Prince, I can confirm that things have not improved in the department."

"With Officer Whitley?" I whisper back.

"Yes. She's...shes's..."

"Intimidating?"

He guffaws. "Me? Intimidated? No, nothing like that. She's just not really a team player. That's why you're here. You are a team player, Rosi."

I don't for a minute believe that Officer Daniel is not threatened by Officer Whitley, but I don't tell him so. Instead, I take his complement. "Glad I can help." I open my water bottle and take a long drink.

"Here!" Dan chucks a snack bag of mini pretzels in my direction which I catch with my left hand.

"Thanks."

"I cued the tape to start a little after 8:00 yesterday morning, the day of the murder."

As if I could forget. "What shall I be looking for?"

"Anything that looks out of place, unusual. People that shouldn't be there. That kind of thing. You were on site every day according to what you've told me, at least part of each day. Right?"

"That's right. Go ahead. Let's take a look."

Officer Daniel pushes the play button. The security camera we'd moved from the back hallway of the senior center now hangs on the outside of our building facing the tech center, but the footage is poor in quality at such a far distance from the building. I already feel defeated. If we don't solve this murder, then the site might stay shut down, pushing out our project completion date.

"Who are the people?" Officer Dan pulls out a yellow legal pad. Good, he's going to take notes. He *does* have notepads.

I point to the screen. "You already know Jakob, of course. The woman with the braid is Gabby. She's one of the construction workers. One of the men she's talking to is Andy. Sorry, I don't know his last name. He's a regular on the job, too, along with that guy, Ross." I point to the two young men talking to Gabby. She looks small standing in between them, though she's no wimp on the job. "Andy is the blonde guy. He walks with a limp. Gabby told me he'd been injured on a job site once, something about a beam falling on his leg and crushing it."

"Ouch!" Dan winces.

"Yeah. The brown-haired guy is Ross. He's not much older than my son Zak, but he's a hard worker. In fact, he's one of the only workers out there that I actually heard Brent Heath give a compliment to."

"What did he say?"

"He said he's never seen someone walk a steel beam faster and with more finesse than Ross."

"That's kind of a cruel thing to say when one of his co-workers has a bum leg."

"I thought the same thing considering Andy was standing right next to him when he dished out the compliment."

"Who are those men?" Officer Dan points to two people who have walked into the camera's view. They pick up paint cans and walk toward a scaffolding set up on the outside of the tech center. They apply safety harnesses before getting onto the scaffolding.

"Painters, obviously. I don't know them."

"I'll make a note to ask Jakob for more information."

I feel like a voyeur watching Gabby, Andy, and Ross finish odd jobs. Most of the outside of the building is complete except for the painting, so they seem to be running around the site picking up loose wires and tubing and various other things. When they move off camera it's in the direction of the virtual reality end of the building which is the only part of the structure not completed. Today Jakob nailed plywood to that end of the building so that no one could vandalize.

"Wait! Who's that?" Officer Dan rewinds the video.

I squint at the screen. On the periphery of the camera shot I see Jade. She's talking to Brent. It's the first time Brent has appeared on the screen.

"It looks like Jade is angry about something. She looks like she's yelling at Brent."

"Lots of finger wagging," he says. "But she looks pretty cute in those work boots," he says with a smarmy smile.

"Dan!"

"Look, there," Officer Daniel points to the middle of the screen where Gabby and Andy are standing over a mesh of wires which look like they are part of a garbage-collecting pile. Gabby pulls out a pair of gloves, grabs handfuls of wire out of the pile, and drops to her knees. She looks from side to side as if looking for someone, but the only one I can see near her at this time is Andy.

"What's she doing on the other side of that pile?" Officer Daniel asks.

"I don't know." We watch Andy walk off camera and return with a large shovel in his hands. He steps in front of Gabby and begins digging, piles of dirt seen flying from behind the collection of wires and debris.

Looking around one last time—and satisfied that Jade and Brent are too involved to notice them—Gabby hands some sort of large box to Andy. She picks up a tarp of some sort from the ground and throws it over the box in Andy's hands as he walks quickly off-site.

"That looks suspicious."

"It sure as heck does," says Officer Daniel. "Do you know anything about that box?"

"Me? I don't know anything."

"How well do you know that woman?"

"Gabby? We met in book club last month. We're reading *Me, Myself Loves Me, Myself*."

"Is it any good?"

"Gabby thinks it's amazing. Apparently, her sister-in-law is as narcissistic as the antagonist so she can relate. I think the antagonist is a lot like Brenda Riker. I imagine poor George had enough and that's why he left."

"George Riker left Brenda?" Officer Daniel asks. "That's news to me."

"You must have missed the memo. It's all over town. But back to the matter at hand, I'll talk to Gabby tonight. I'm picking her up for our meeting at Caliope Davento's house."

"Caliope?"

"Yeah, she's a teacher at the middle school. Do you know her?"

"I...I know her a little. A few weeks ago, I talked to her students about cyber safety. She's real pretty."

Dan turns away from me so that I don't see the red blotches appearing, an assortment of little raspberries on his face. "Dan, do you have a crush on a school teacher?"

"Stop it, Rosi. I don't have a crush." He rubs his hands together with nervous energy and reaches for my empty pretzel bag, knocking my open water bottle over in the process.

I grab the tissue box on his desk and start blotting the water with tissues before it soaks his yellow legal pad. "You should ask her out, Dan. She might say yes."

"Let's finish watching the video footage." He clicks play on the laptop, and a few minutes after Andy has walked away with the box, Brent Heath approaches Gabby since Jade has gone into the tech center. There is no volume, so we can't make out what they are saying, but he's talking very near her face, so close that she pushes him away and he stumbles before catching his footing. More yelling and angry faces until Gabby turns on the heel of her work boot and walks out of the view of the camera. Brent kicks dirt back into the hole with his boots. Nothing more out of the ordinary happens as Officer Daniel fast forwards. The video abruptly stops at 6:00 p.m. "When did the day usually end for the workers?"

"It depended. Sometimes the crew would still be working when I left at 5:00. Sometimes they clocked out at 4:30."

"I think I need to talk to Jakob," says Dan as he clicks off the monitor.

"I'll get back to you after I've talked to Gabby."

"Yes. I'd talk to her myself, but with you seeing her tonight and having a relationship already, you make the logical interviewer."

"Or perhaps you'd like Officer Whitley to question Gabby, since she's a police officer and all?" I roll my eyes, but Officer Daniel completely misses my sarcasm.

"No. I think you will do."

"Thanks for the compliment," I say, dryly. I stand up to leave. "I'll be in touch." Before I walk out of his office, I turn back. Dan is wiping pretzel crumbs off his uniform sleeves. "Ask Caliope out. The worst thing that might happen is that she'd say no."

"Don't forget the public humiliation of being turned down by a *school teacher.*"

"Throw shade like that at our humble public servants and you deserve every bit of humiliation you'd receive. Behave Officer Dan Daniel. Behave."

Chapter 8

I return to my office for the last hour of the day. Tracy is meeting with Jakob in a closed door meeting, so I don't interrupt. My role in the Roland Price Technology Center project has been mostly as a supportive number two to Tracy. That, and marketing. Right now all of my big marketing campaigns and media announcements are on hold until we get a final date for completion. I will pad the time because problems always come up in construction, but with a murder investigation shutting down our site, I have no idea how long we will be delayed. Late October is the target for our grand opening. Ribbon cutting, champagne bottle smashed across the side of the building because Bob Horace had insisted we do that even though Brenda had argued to *keep it classy*. Bob doesn't ask for a lot, so I'd chosen his side much to Brenda's displeasure. I've come to realize that she dislikes any idea that is not her own. I wonder what trauma happened to her in her younger years to turn her into a fiery narcissist. I think I'll donate my book club book to her when I'm done reading, although can a true narcissist appreciate a book *about* a narcissist? I imagine not. Brenda likely doesn't realize how maddening she is to everyone else.

The nagging issue of the security system being shut off at 6:00 p.m. on the night of Brent's murder leads me to the closet that houses the security technology. Tracy had been so proud when she'd purchased the system a month after Sherman Padowski's death. We all knew it was Sherman's death and a lack of working cameras in the auditorium that prompted the purchase, but it was time to modernize, too—way past time. I enter the tiny closet that holds the security monitoring system. A computer monitor features views from the three active cameras: the camera by the front door of the senior center, the camera with a view of the auditorium and stage, and the camera that used to view the backdoor entrance of the senior center and now focuses on the closed-down construction site. It's been turned back on though nothing is happening there at the moment. There are no police officers scouring for clues. There is no construction crew finishing the state-of-the-art project.

I am wondering if anyone thought to check for fingerprints on the monitor when I spy some dirt on the floor that hadn't been hit with Mario's mop yet. I reach into my purse and pull out a tissue, but just before I swipe away the dirt, I notice the outline of a shoeprint, an interesting outline made by a very narrow shoe with a small circle not much bigger than a quarter marking the back of the shoe. It's a shoeprint from a high heel shoe. Tracy, Mario, and I are the only ones who access this room, and the killer perhaps, I realize. Does the killer wear high heels? Instead of wiping away the shoeprint, I snap a close-up picture and text it to Officer Daniel.

On my way home, I pick up six tacos to go from my favorite Mexican take-out restaurant. Keaton meets me at the door of his condo with a giant grin on his face. "There's my girl." He gives me a hug before giving me a funny look and pointing to the tacos. "Are you sure your stomach is settled enough for tacos?"

"Oops, yeah, right. I didn't even think about that." I wrinkle my nose in contemplation. "Maybe I'll try one taco and see how I feel. I only have an hour before I have to pick up Gabby for book club."

"I never would have believed you had I not seen it myself that your friendship with Gabby began at a book club. She doesn't seem the reading type."

"Apparently I'm not the reading type, either, considering I only had time to skim read my chapters for tonight." I open the bag of tacos and set them out on the kitchen island.

"You can be forgiven. You've been a little busy."

"Hear ye! Hear ye!" I yell through my cupped hands around my mouth. "Rosi Laruee has stumbled upon yet another dead body!"

"You should write a book for book club."

I laugh. "Yes, I'm a regular Jessica Fletcher."

"Naw, you're a lot cuter than Jessica Fletcher." He takes a strand of my hair that has come loose from my bun and tucks it behind my ears. "Do we have time for anything else besides tacos?" he asks, his eyes twinkling with naughtiness.

"You are incorrigible, Alex P. Keaton."

"Give me your inner Blanche, and I'll show you how incorrigible I am." He throws his head back in laugher before picking me up and carrying me into his bedroom.

Gabby slides into my front seat within seconds of me pulling into the parking lot of her apartment building. She's wearing a red and black plaid ¾ sleeved shirt, blue jeans, and cowboy boots. Her normally braided hair is brushed out, a long, black mane of hair falling down her back. She's an exotic beauty and a bit of a chameleon who can move from construction worker to model-ready with a mere shower and hair brushing. If only I could be so lucky, I think, as I look in the rearview mirror, wishing I'd reapplied my eye makeup after leaving Keaton's before running home to let Barley out to pee. At least I'd put on clean jeans and a new yellow t-shirt. I know I'll be bombarded with questions, so I'd chosen a sunny yellow color to improve my mood.

"Hey, Rosi. How's it going?"

"It's going."

"Yeah, kind of a crap day for sure. I still can't believe that someone would off Brent Heath like that. I mean, the guy was worse than a bully, but murder's a step too far, right?"

"Uh, yeah, I think that would be a fair assessment."

"Do you have any idea who'd do that?"

"I have no idea." I chew the inside of my cheek, contemplating how to broach the next question. "Gabby, Officer Daniel and I were watching security footage today from yesterday's work day."

"Oh man! You caught Brent's murder on camera? Gnarly!"

"No, no. I wish. I mean, not that I wish I could have *seen* it happen, but just that it would be nice to have this solved so we can get back to work."

"And so Brent's family can get some peace," she says, giving me a judgmental eye.

"Oh my gosh! Of course. I didn't mean to be so detached. I've seen a lot this year. I guess I'm getting immune to the effects of murder." I shudder at this realization and refocus my thoughts. "Look, Gabby. I'm going to be honest with you. Officer Daniel and I saw you arguing with Brent."

"Really?"

"It looked like a heated exchange."

"Hmm…"

"You can tell me, Gabby."

She sighs loudly. "I know. It's stupid. He was hitting on me, and I wasn't interested. It's just a boring story."

"Oh. We also saw you and Andy in the footage covering up some kind of box—and Andy carrying it away. What's up with that box?"

I see Gabby through my peripheral vision sink lower into my passenger seat. "You saw that?"

"We did. Officer Daniel will be asking you about it, too."

"Oh." She takes a long, slow, deep breath.

"Andy and I were prepping the ground for the pouring of the concrete next week for the sidewalks when we hit on something hard in the ground."

"The box?"

"Yeah. It was buried about two feet under the ground."

"Did you tell anyone?"

"No. We promised that we'd keep it between the two of us."

"What was inside the box, Gabby?"

"Beer."

"Beer?"

"Yep. Old beer. In glass bottles." She looks out the window.

"What else was in the box? I know you're being evasive, and I don't get it, Gabby."

"Fine. I'll tell you. And I'll tell Officer Daniel, but it doesn't make Andy or me look very good."

"Okay. The truth is almost always best."

"I know. We should have told someone right when we opened the box. Maybe it was the thrill of a find that only the two of us knew about."

"Do you and Andy have some kind of relationship, other than as co-workers, that I don't know about?"

"Andy? Heck, no! Have you seen that guy's fingernails? They are disgusting, Rosi. Years of caked in dirt, and he bites them, too. Eww!" She scrunches up her face and shudders. "We were together when we found the box. That's our only connection."

"Gabby, what else was in the box?" She doesn't answer. Instead, she stares out the window as we drive out of town toward Caliope's house, our bottles of unopened wine clanking together in the backseat.

"There was a key."

"A key?"

"Yeah, one of those old timey keys like you'd find in an old house. But Andy thinks the key opens a lock, not a door."

"What kind of lock?"

"I'm not sure."

"So, all that was in the box was old beer and a key?"

"No, there was more."

"Well, spit it out, girl. We are almost at Caliope's house." I tighten my grip on the steering wheel, growing irritated with Gabby's coyness.

"There was a brick."

"What kind of brick?"

"Not an adobe brick or a common house brick, but a cinder block."

"The heavy kind?"

"I don't know of a light cinder block."

"Okay, so old beer, an old key, and a cinder block?"

"A black cinder block. And…oh, look, there's Caliope's house!"

"And, *what?* I'm going to keep driving if you don't spit it out."

"Fine! There was five thousand dollars in $100 bills or half of that at least."

"Half of that?"

"Yeah, there were fifty $100 bills ripped in half."

"Did you tape them together?" I can feel my heartbeat increasing, recognizing the greed of my new friend.

"Nope."

"Oh." Maybe she's not so greedy after all.

"There was literally *one half* of every $100 bill. The matching halves were missing."

"Missing?"

"You know, not there?"

"I know what *missing* means. What did you do with everything?"

"Andy and I each cracked open a Pabst Blue Ribbon beer bottle and toasted to our unluckiness. I can report that the flavor of a 1985 PBR isn't that different from a PBR in the 2020s."

"Wow." I pull in front of Caliope's ranch home behind a large SUV belonging to a soccer mom.

"You see? It was a very boring story," says Gabby. "Sorry it didn't solve your murder. I wish I could have helped. And I wish that stash of money had been complete."

"Would you have kept it? The money?"

Gabby shrugs her shoulders. "There *is* the expression *finders' keepers*."

"I guess." But what I am really thinking is, *that wasn't your property you were digging in—so it wasn't your box—so that'd be stealing*. I keep the thoughts to myself.

Chapter 9

Caliope's home is nothing like I'd expected. Why I continue to stereotype teachers this long in my years I am not sure. There are no #1 teacher mugs on the counters or newly crocheted blankets on the back of the couch. No children's books on the coffee table or homemade knickknacks, gifts from students past. The kitchen is stark white with gold-colored accessories. The furniture in the living room features a purple couch that somehow compliments the mustard-colored chair across from it so well that I'm contemplating an update in my own furniture. The only thing that even remotely makes this house look like its owner is a teacher is its small size. No large pay checks for Caliope. Good gracious, what would her house design look like if she had more room in which to decorate?

"Rosi, I am surprised to see you," says Caliope as we settle on the purple couch, wine glasses full.

"Why? I haven't missed a book club in the last two months," I say, taking a sip of my wine.

"I know that," she says, her widely-spaced large eyes staring at me. She tucks a lock of her auburn hair behind her ear. "I heard about what happened in Tucson Valley. You must be traumatized."

"You, too, Gabby," says Helena Bourder, the owner of the bakery in town, the one next to Salem's Stories Bookstore that is now called Tucson Reads.

"Me? I'm fine. Hey, I get a few days off work!" Gabby laughs as she downs her glass of wine.

"Interesting take," says Caliope as she turns to me. "Ginger and Jordan Beacher were absent today," she says, picking up a bowl of homemade trail mix and passing it around the room.

"Who are Ginger and Jordan Beacher?" I ask.

"The twins of Jakob Beacher. Isn't he your foreman on the tech center project?"

"General contractor. His kids go to your school?"

"Yep. They are in my sixth grade math class. Great kiddos. It seems, according to their mom, that Jakob has been distraught with grief all day. She kept them home to cheer him up, to distract him."

"Oh, wow. I didn't know he felt such a connection to Brent."

"On another note, have any of you seen that hunky architect that's been around Tucson Valley this week? Oohla-la. He is hot!" says Helena, her short hairdo bobbing on her head as she talks animatedly. "He was in my bakery yesterday. Be still my little heart!"

"What did he buy?" asks Gabby. "He's not my type. Too much of a meathead."

I try not to laugh as Gabby is like the female version of Oliver with long hair and a gorgeous body.

"Well, some lady may have gotten lucky. He bought a heart-shaped cookie with my homemade buttercream frosting. And I'd drawn an arrow over the frosting."

"Like Cupid's arrow?" Caliope asks, clutching her heart, her wide eyes growing impossibly wider with awe.

"Just like that," says Helena.

"He's not my type, either," says Caliope coyly.

I take the bait. "Who's your type, Caliope?"

"You will all laugh at me if I tell you."

"We won't laugh! We promise," say Helena.

"Whoever it is would be stupid to not jump at a chance to date the great Caliope Davento," says Gabby.

Caliope looks at each of us carefully, as if considering whether or not to continue. "I'll tell you." She takes a deep breath as Gabby, Helena, and I lean in closer. "Officer Daniel," she says quietly.

"What?" asks Gabby, immediately throwing a hand over her mouth. "Sorry. Sorry! I am not laughing. I am *not* laughing."

"See! I knew I never should have said a thing." She pouts like a teenager who's just been told that she can't stay out past curfew.

I put a hand on Caliope's shoulder until she turns back around. "Dan is cool. There's a lot more to him than his exterior."

"That's not much more helpful, Rosi!" she cries.

"No, no, that sounded bad. I wasn't talking about his nose, I mean, his personal appearance." I see Gabby cover her mouth again so she doesn't laugh. "What I *meant*, is that sometimes he puts on an air of confidence about himself that can be *off-putting*—"

"Not helpful."

"But it's an act, Caliope. He's just a vulnerable human being like all of us, and he has the best intentions in what he's doing. There's a lot under the surface that's really positive. It will take a special person to bring that out, and you are that person, Caliope."

"Thank you, Rosi—I think."

"When did you set your sights on Officer Daniel?" asks Helena as she refills her wine glass.

"He came to our school and talked to the kids about cyber safety. He was very friendly."

"I bet he was."

"Gabby!" I yell as Helena throws a pillow at her.

"Sorry!"

"Caliope, I knew about the school assembly," I say, my chance to be helpful.

"How did you know?"

"Because Officer Daniel told me—today."

"Why did he tell you?" Her eyes sparkle with a hint of expectation at my answer.

"When he and I were talking about the, uh, *case*, I told him I was coming to your house for book club."

"Speaking of, do you think we will actually talk about the book today?" asks Gabby.

"Not likely," says Helena.

"Anyway, he told me about meeting you and said that you were pretty."

"He did?" Caliope touches her hair and grins. "That's nice."

"We can double date!" says Helena.

"Who's your date?" I ask.

"Naturally, the hunky architect. Duh!"

We collapse into a fit of laughter in Caliope's trendy living room, trying to avoid smashing into the glass coffee table. It's nice to have friends in Tucson Valley, friends that are contemporaries, even if I'm the only one who's reached 40. Sometimes I forget that I'm not quite heading to retirement yet when I spend so much time with people who are fifteen to thirty years older.

We spend a half hour talking about the *Me, Myself Loves Me, Myself* book. We skip the questions in our book study guide to talk about the hunky lead and his undeserving mistress. As the clock nears 9:00, I realize how tired I am, physically and mentally. Gabby reads my face and finishes her fourth glass of wine. I'd stopped after one. I'd be asleep on top of the coffee table if I'd had four glasses of wine.

Before Gabby gets out of the car when we get back to her apartment building, I remind her that I want to see the contents of the box she and Andy took from the construction site, preferably before Officer Daniel sees them. I want to see if the items inside make sense when I'm seeing them with my own eyes before they go to the police.

"Tomorrow, Rosi. Tomorrow. I've got a mad headache."

"I wonder why," I say sarcastically.

"What was that?"

"Nothing. Do you need help getting into your apartment?"

"No, thanks. As long as a javelina doesn't jump out in front of me, I think I can make it." She smiles, but her eyes barely open.

"Get some sleep, Gabby. I'll call you tomorrow."

"Oh, Rosi!" she says before she shuts the car door. "Do you remember that snake skin I showed you?"

"I remember."

"That little critter's still out there. I know it cause I saw his den. I didn't want to freak ya out. Be careful."

"Awesome. Maybe we can become acquainted." I don't smile. Gabby shuts the door. I wait until she is in her apartment before leaving. I make a mental note to call whomever you're supposed to call to exterminate rattlesnakes from their natural habitat.

Chapter 10

Tracy texted me this morning to stop by her office first thing for a big announcement. I text Gabby that I will come over during my lunch break to look at the box before she takes it to the police station this afternoon.

I take Barley to work with me this morning. I won't be out on the construction site, and fewer people will be around, so she won't have to dodge any hazards. Plus, maybe she'll give me an advanced warning of our phantom snake.

"Barley!" I let go of her leash as she runs into Tracy's office. "Who's a good girl?" Tracy rubs Barley's face and ears. Barley rewards her with a sloppy kiss across the nose. "I missed you, too, girl."

"Rosi, have a seat. I want to show you something."

I sit across from Tracy. When Barley has received the proper amount of loving, she settles in a heap at my feet. "What do you have to show me?"

"Jakob and I had a long meeting yesterday. He's so torn up over this project being delayed."

"And about Brent Heath's murder, I presume?"

"Well, of course. That goes without saying. Personalities aside, a murder is a murder, and it's just awful.

Two murders on our property this year! Can you believe it?" She sinks back into her chair as we sit silently contemplating this crazy reality.

"So, we put our heads together to come up with something positive."

"Okay." Sometimes Tracy's ideas scare me like when she had Mario and I hang Christmas lights over the auditorium seating to *give off a pleasing ambiance* before performances, but the lighting was so poor we had guests tripping over themselves and each other to such a catastrophic effect that Vickie from Jackie's Boutique broke her big toe.

"Plus, this idea will save money. Do you remember that big sculpture that Jade revealed she was going to hang in the entryway of the tech center?"

"The one with the history of computers? In metal?"

"Yes, that one."

"What about it?" I already have a negative view of that overly abstract piece of *art*.

"We are going to cancel the order. It will save us money…"

"Great idea!" I say before realizing that she isn't done talking.

"And we are going to hold a contest. We will commission the painting of a mural on the wall inside the entryway, something that will be welcoming and inclusive and highlight the incredibly important advancement in technology centers for the aging population in our community."

"Wow. I think that's an incredible idea, Tracy."

She claps her hands like an excited toddler who's been told she can stay up for one more story. "I hoped you would like it! What I need you to do is put together the plan in writing and spread the news—quickly—so that the painting can be completed by opening day, whenever that may be."

"I can do that. I'd love something positive to work on. Anything else?"

"No, no. Get to work on this right away."

"On it, Captain," I salute Tracy and reach for Barley's leash.

"Can she stay a little longer? I really enjoy her company."

"No problem." I turn to go but then remember the matter I needed to discuss with her. "Tracy, do you know what happened to your work boots?"

"What do you mean?"

"They haven't been on the mat by the back door since the night that Brent was, uh, found."

"I hadn't noticed. I've been wearing these old tennis shoes," she says, kicking up her leg on her desk and showing me a pair of blue Nikes. "They are so much more comfortable than those heavy work boots. I guess that's why I didn't realize they were missing. Who would steal my work boots?"

"I have no idea. Huh. Well, I'll keep an eye out for them. I'll get the ball rolling on the mural project. And…and you might want to investigate what to do about a western diamondback rattlesnake den."

"What?"

"Just ask around!" I close her office door before she can ask more questions.

I spend the rest of the morning working on the media I will release about the commission of the mural for our tech center. The requirements? Convey the mission of the tech center to offer opportunities to all residents of Tucson Valley Retirement Community that will promote the ability to continue their education later into life, open lines of communication with people around the world, and enhance the day-to-day quality of life with interesting and enriching experiences. And be fast. The idea has to be sketched, voted on, and completed within a few short weeks. I email Tracy my ideas and leave the senior center to meet with Gabby and view the contents of the box she and Andy had discovered at the construction site.

Gabby is waiting for me in the parking lot outside the local library. I get out of my car and into hers. Her eyes are bloodshot. Did she continue drinking when she got home? "You look like you've had a rough night," I say, squeezing her hand so she knows I'm supportive.

When she looks up at me, a line of tears slides down her face, silent crying, some of the most painful kind of tears. "Gabby! What happened?"

"He took the box."

"Who took the box?"

"Last night, as soon as you left, there was a knock on my door. He must have been waiting for me to get home. I thought it was you, that you'd forgotten to tell me something. And when I opened the door, he barged right in. I'm a tough girl, Rosi, but I didn't have much fight in me last night after all that wine. Why did I drink so much wine?"

"Gabby, you're skipping an important detail. Who was at your door? Who took the box?"

"Andy."

"Why would he take it? He'd been the one to let you hold on to it, right?"

"Right."

"I get that you found the box together, but why'd he take it back from you?"

"I texted him last night—from Caliope's house—after I told you about the box. I guess I felt like I owed it to him that I'd told you the truth. He didn't want me to give the box to Officer Daniel. Said he could frame me for Brent Heath's death if I told anyone about the box. That's why I'm meeting you here." She looks out the car windows, panning the area for any sign of trouble.

"How on earth could he frame you for Brent's death?"

"Because I can't find my nail gun."

"What do you mean?"

"My nail gun is missing."

"So?" Then the reality of what Gabby is saying hits me like a ton of the cinder blocks found inside that box.

"The police don't know whose nail gun was used to kill Brent. What if it was my nail gun, Rosi? What if Andy has my nail gun? Then I'd look guilty. But I'm not guilty, Rosi. I didn't kill Brent Heath. He was an arrogant bully, but I didn't kill him. I just ignored him. Most of the time I have pretty thick skin—most of the time."

"Oh, Gabby. I'm so sorry. I wish you had called me last night."

Gabby sniffles as if she's trying to keep from crying. "I couldn't risk it. Andy was possessed like a wild animal. I'd never seen him like that."

"Did he hurt you, Gabby? Did Andy hurt you?" I can feel my own anger rising through my body as I contemplate my new friend being harmed.

"No, not physically. He yelled a lot, got in my face. Called me all kinds of nasty names. Called me a traitor."

"I'm so sorry," I say again. "Why does he want that box so badly?"

"I don't know. Maybe he knows where the other half of that money is. Maybe he wants money. Maybe he killed Brent. Nothing makes sense anymore."

"Why would Andy have killed Brent?"

Gabby looks at me and cocks her head to the side. "Don't you know about the accident?"

"The accident?"

"Andy's leg was crushed a few years ago in a site accident. A beam came loose and caught his leg. He had to have three surgeries to repair the damage, and he's still getting physical therapy. The accident left him with a permanent limp."

"Yeah, I've noticed, but what does that have to do with Brent Heath?"

"Brent was the construction manager in charge of the job site. He'd ok'd the placement of a steel column minutes before the column came loose causing the beam to fall. He's lucky his chest wasn't pinned under the beam or he'd have lost his life. He holds Brent responsible to this day."

I stare out the windshield of my car taking in everything Gabby has just told me. "We have to tell Officer Daniel."

"Rosi, no! If Andy *did* kill Brent and I rat him out, he's coming after me, especially if I told Officer Daniel about the box, too."

"So, you want to let a possible murderer loose for life to off the next person that he perceives does him wrong?"

"No. Stop it. I know you're right," she sighs. "Fine. But give me an hour. I'm all packed up," she says, pointing to her bag in the back of the car. "I'm going to go to my sister's place in Scottsdale and lie low until we figure out Andy's reaction after Officer Daniel confronts him. But you have to be the one to tell the police. Can you do that for me, Rosi?"

"I don't like it. You should be the one. You are the firsthand source. But I also understand your hesitation. I'll do it." I straighten my shoulders. "In one hour."

"Thanks, Rosi." Gabby reaches across the front seat console to hug me, her grasp so strong I feel like *I'm* being crushed under a beam.

Chapter 11

I text Tracy that I'm going to be late for work this afternoon and that we might have a new lead in the investigation. The faster this case is solved, the faster we can finish the technology center. Officer Whitley groans when she sees me enter the police station before she returns to reading whatever is on her computer monitor that is more important than greeting me. I walk past her to Officer Daniel's office without so much as a wave.

I catch Officer Daniel up on my conversation with Gabby about Andy and the contents of the box found on site. He listens carefully without interruption. When I am done talking, he holds his hands together and stretches his arms out in front of him and nods his head up and down.

"Well, what do you think?" I finally ask, his silence both odd and annoying.

"I think you've been duped."

"What?" Unkind thoughts about Officer Daniel spin around in my mind faster that a dryer set to high heat. I may have become an amateur sleuth by accident, but I'm good at what I do.

"Mr. Carmen has an airtight alibi."

"And how do you know this?" I ball my hands into fists, frustrated that I may have been wrong about this case.

"Because his wife came to me yesterday to tell me that he'd actually quit his job the afternoon that Mr. Heath was murdered."

"That doesn't mean anything—if it's even true. He could have gone back to the site to kill him. From what Gabby's told us, we know he harbored resentment toward Brent."

"She said they'd gone away to celebrate."

"To celebrate her husband *quitting a job?* That's dumb. It doesn't sound right at all. And what proof is there?"

"Rosi, Rosi, Rosi," Officer Daniel says, rotating his head from side to side. "You must accept that you don't know everything. You haven't earned the wisdom from years of experience like I have."

"Dan, you didn't know anything about the past connection between Andy and Brent until I told you fifteen minutes ago. Deflate that ego a bit."

He laughs. "Fine, but I *did* look for alibis of everyone who was at the job site, and Andy and his wife *did* go away the night of the murder. I have hotel security footage of them checking in *and* restaurant security footage of them eating dinner during the time Mr. Heath met his most unfortunate demise."

"Oh." I sink a little lower in my seat.

"Don't feel so bad, Rosi." He reaches across the desk to pat my hand like a parent mockingly comforting a child about losing a Barbie shoe or Hot Wheels car, something so insignificant in the scope of life. But to the child? Everything.

"But you didn't know about the contents of the box!" I shoot back, now sounding like a bratty teenager. I need to get myself under control.

"I did not. But I don't think the box has anything to do with Mr. Heath. After all, none of the money was intact. It's useless."

"Unless he knew where the other half was."

"Don't get all crazy, Rosi. But I appreciate your effort."

I stand up to leave before I say something I might regret later. My head pounds with frustration.

"Wait! There was *one* good thing you brought to my attention."

I stare at him in silence until he continues, not giving him any hint of craving information.

"That shoeprint you found in the security closet? It was definitely from a high heel. I'm heading out to talk to Jade about it this evening. I have a dentist appointment first. Want to come with me? Like old times? Not to the dentist, though," he laughs at himself.

I want to say no. I want to say *hell no* after the way he humiliated me about my theory of Andy's guilt in this case, but I can't. I need to follow this investigation to the end, however many leads there may be. And this one leads to Jade.

"I'll meet you." I turn on the heel of my dirty gray sneakers and walk out of the office and the police station as quickly as I can. The only thing giving me glee is that I didn't tell him about Caliope's interest. That can wait.

Barley is completely sprawled out on top of Tracy's desk when I go to retrieve her. It's quite a sight to see a fifty-pound dog laying across your boss's desk. "How on earth are you even getting any work done?" I laugh.

"Oh, that," she giggles. "Barley really wanted to be close, and my lap isn't big enough for her anymore, so I cleared off my desk. I can still access my computer. It's all good."

Barley looks at me and barks as if to say, *I've got this, Mom. Leave me be.*

"Her first puppy obedience class is later tonight. Goodness knows she needs it. I've waited much too long."

Barley barks again and doesn't stop until Tracy pulls a treat from her desk drawer and hands it to her. "She's certainly trained *me* well."

"Do you want me to leave her here or take her back to my office?"

"Please leave her here. We have a great working relationship. Don't we, Barley?" She pets Barley under her chin until she rolls over onto her back for belly rubs. What a spoiled animal.

When I get back to my office, I call Keaton. He answers after four rings, out of breath. "Hey, Rosi."

"Keaton? Sorry. Were you in the middle of something?"

"Yeah, we're raking leaves at the historic mansion property outside of the retirement community. They have a surprising number of trees that have survived decades in the Arizona desert."

"The property that the board went to court over trying to get the owner to deed the land back to the retirement community? I heard something like that when I started working here."

"I don't know all of the details, but from what I heard, the mansion used to be considered part of the Tucson Valley Retirement Community land, but when the Grayson family bought the house and lot in the 80s, they petitioned the city of Tucson Valley to separate the property from TVRC and to rezone it as part of the city proper."

"Why?"

"To avoid paying HOA dues, I guess. And to avoid having to live by the laws of the board. It makes sense, though. The house looks nothing like most of the other buildings in the retirement community."

"True."

"So, what's up?"

"Oh, yeah, sorry. This may seem out of left field, but has Oliver mentioned anything to you about being interested in someone local?"

"Like, in the retirement community?" He laughs so strong and with an air of sweetness that my heart melts a little.

"No, not like retirement age, you nut. Well, specifically, do you think that Oliver has a thing for Jade?"

"The interior designer?"

"Yeah."

"He hasn't shared anything like that with me. Want me to ask him?"

"No. Don't say anything, at least not now. Have fun with your leaves."

"Thanks. Any chance I can see your beautiful face tonight?"

"I doubt it. Barley has her puppy class, and Officer Daniel and I have a meeting. I'll tell you about it later."

"If I didn't know better, I'd think you were spending a little too much time with Officer Daniel because you're sweet on him."

"Ugh. You'll make me throw up again. I'll call ya later. Bye!"

A knock on my office door surprises me. "Hey, Rosi."

Mario is holding Barley's leash as she licks his shoes. "Tracy was on her way out, and I told her I'd drop Barley off at your office."

"Thanks, Mario. Sorry about the shoes."

"It's okay. They're waterproof."

I smile. "I've been wondering about something, Mario."

"What's that?" He strokes his gray beard as if readying for a tough question.

"Is there any chance that the security camera wasn't actually off when the murder occurred but that the footage was erased?"

"Huh, well, I can check the manual that the installer gave me when he put in the system. Now that you mention it, there was some talk about the cloud keeping footage, but to me the word *cloud* and technology don't belong in the same sentence. You know what I mean?"

"I know. Can you check on that for me, please? When you get a chance? I need to take Barley to her puppy obedience class."

"Holy moly! Good luck with that." He's still shaking his head back and forth as Barley and I follow him out the door.

Chapter 12

It doesn't take coaxing to get Barley out of my car and into the doggie daycare center where the puppy obedience class is being held. She's always up for an adventure. However, at the front door we meet an older woman who isn't as keen on Barley as most people. The woman, with a knit cap on her head as if it's a Midwest fall evening and not a Tucson fall evening, is holding a chihuahua in her arms. As I'm putting my phone in my purse, Barley jumps on the woman's legs, startling her. She drops the chihuahua that then begins to race across the parking lot.

"Tito! Tito!" She glares at me before running after her dog.

"Barley, no!" Barley barrels after Tito, breaking free from the leash. I follow in pursuit, running after Barley who is running after Tito with his owner who is falling behind.

A man I presume to be the teacher comes outside when he hears our hollering. He cuts Tito off before he runs down an alley on the side of the building and picks him up just as I regain control of Barley's leash. The woman and I are both out of breath. "I'm so sorry. I really am."

"You need to get that dog under control. My poor Tito could have been run over by a car!" The wrinkles between her eyes deepen into a V that make her look both old and evil at the same time.

"I know." Barley plops herself onto the sidewalk outside the building, too exhausted to move. I have to pull a treat from my pocket to get her up.

The teacher looks at me and shakes his head in judgement.

After class, which consisted of Barley coming in last place in the *leave it* exercises, I take her home, dejected. But *I* would have had a hard time leaving a piece of steak on the ground, too, if it were just sitting there tempting me. Still, I should have taken her to classes months ago. Too many dead bodies piling up and keeping me from my responsibilities, I guess.

I pull out my phone to text Officer Daniel.

I'm free to go with you to see Jade.
Great. She's staying at the Desert Tumbleweed Inn.
Okay. I'll meet you in the parking lot in fifteen minutes.

I drive to the Desert Tumbleweed Inn, a short drive outside of the retirement community. The senior center had paid for a few nights of Jade's stay in Tucson Valley when she'd come into town for meetings, but I don't really understand why she's still here. Maybe she thinks that the police will figure things out or at least reopen the site so she can finish with whatever design work she needs to do before returning to California.

"Did you tell her we were coming?" I ask Officer Daniel when we meet outside the lobby of the hotel.

"No. Should I have?"

"I don't know. Is there a surprise element to your questioning about her shoeprint being in the security closet?"

"No. Maybe. I don't know."

I roll my eyes and rub my temples. "Do you even have a line of questioning for Jade?"

"Kind of. Maybe? I'm going to tell her that I know she was in the security closet, that I think *she* was the one who shut off the camera."

"If you believe that, then you must think she is the one who killed Brent Heath."

"Hmm. It does kind of sound like that, doesn't it?"

"Duh. And how do you even know it was Jade's high heels that made that shoeprint and not somebody else's fancy shoes?"

"Do you know anyone else who wore fancy shoes like that around a construction site?"

"No. I do not. Do you know her room number at least?"

Dan pulls out a piece of paper from his pocket. "Room 323. I called Tracy to ask her. She said the senior center has been putting her and Oliver up in hotel rooms while they were in town for work."

"I didn't realize Oliver was staying here, too. I guess that makes sense."

We enter the lobby. Officer Daniel talks with the young woman at the front desk. She looks terrified to have a police officer question her on the job as if this isn't the first time she's been questioned by the police. Her face screams *guilty. But, of what?*

"Let me do the talking," Officer Daniel says when we get off the elevator.

I want to ask why he'd even wanted to bring me along then, but I don't say anything.

He reads the number outside the door to himself. "Room 323. Yep, this is it." Knock, knock, knock. No answer. Knock, knock, knock.

"Who is it?" calls the saccharine sweet voice of Jade from the other side of the door.

"Uh, room service," says Officer Daniel.

"Why?" I whisper, raising my shoulders, my palms opened wide.

"Saw it in the movies," he whispers back. "Trust me."

The door opens. But it's not Jade who is facing us, a look of sheer surprise written in his wide-opened eyes. "Rosi?"

"Oliver?"

"You aren't room service," says Jade, appearing in her hotel robe with her long hair tied into a messy bun on top of her head that manages to make her look even more beautiful than when properly made up.

"Hello, Jade. Mr. Putnam." He tips his hat at them both. "I have a few questions for you," he says dramatically, "about the death of Mr. Brent Heath."

"Why didn't you call? I'd have gladly answered any questions you have."

"This does kind of seem like an ambush," Oliver says, pulling a t-shirt back over his chest, his perfect abs still defined through the fabric of his shirt.

"Ms....Ms. Jade, can we talk alone, please?" He squints his eyes at Oliver.

"My friend can stay. What are your questions?" She frowns as she tightly pulls on the sash of her robe.

"I have one question to start with—an important one.'"

"Go ahead." She sits on the end of the bed with a look of impatience.

Dan takes a deep breath. "We found a shoeprint in the security footage closet, the closet where the security equipment is kept."

Jade raises her eyebrows as if to say, *so what?*

"As I was saying, we found a shoeprint in the dust that had been tracked in from the construction site. There's a lot of dust kicked up on a construction project."

"Duh."

"Anyway, it was the shoeprint from a high-heeled shoe."

"What's your point, Officer Daniel?" Oliver asks. It's the first time I've seen him frown.

"You are the only one who wore high-heeled shoes anywhere near that place." I'm both surprised and proud that Dan speaks so convincingly about something he is *not* convinced of.

Jade nods her head up and down a few times before speaking. "Do you think that I turned off the cameras and then murdered Brent?"

"I don't know. We saw footage of you speaking with him on camera on the site earlier in the day. Neither of you looked very happy."

"And did you happen to notice what shoes I was wearing then?" She puts her hands on her hips.

"Shoes?" he asks.

"You're convinced that I was in that room after yelling at Brent—that I'd decided to kill him and turned off the cameras so I could send nails into this heart a few hours later." Her voice rises with every word she speaks. She marches across the room and comes back a few seconds later. In her hands are a pair of work boots—the work boots that look identical to mine—except mine are on the shoe mat by the back door of the senior center. And Tracy's boots are missing. Only they aren't missing. Because they are in Jade's hands.

"I borrowed these extra work boots from the senior center. There were a couple of pairs for the taking, so I used these when I had to walk in the dirt."

I don't tell Jade that they aren't communal shoes, but I acknowledge to Officer Daniel that we're one pair short at the senior center. "Can you check the tape when you get back to the office?" I ask quietly.

"I can. Ms. Jade, this doesn't let you off the hook. You could still have walked into that closet in your heels."

"I could have done a lot of things," she says dryly.

"And there are many more things I'd rather be *doing* right now."

She runs her hand over Oliver's butt as he smiles. I notice a plastic container with Helena's bakery's name sitting on the dresser next to the television. Of course, the frosted cookie came from Oliver.

"One more thing," Officer Daniel says, trying to dig up as much self-respect as possible. "What were you and Mr. Heath arguing about?"

She rolls her eyes. "I told him that painting the building yellow was a horrendous idea. He told me to go to hell and that he didn't ask for my opinion," she pauses. "You can go now."

I have to bite my tongue not to tell Jade that Tracy and I had chosen the building's color, though I am secretly pleased that Brent had taken our side, at least with Jade, because he'd made it very clear to me that he also hated the color yellow.

"And one more thing," Jade says, the sash on her robe loosening and threatening to reveal her assets. "This stupid contest you've concocted for someone to paint a mural inside the front door of the technology center will prove to be an embarrassment of epic proportions. There is *no* way someone could create something better than the masterpiece I had on order. And only to save money? Shame. Shame. Shame." She tightens her robe again, holding it close to her body. "It's time to go now." Oliver waves goodbye from over Jade's shoulder. I don't wave back.

"That didn't go exactly as planned," Officer Daniel says as we walk out of the hotel's lobby.

"I didn't think you had a plan."

"True."

"Do you think Jade had anything to do with Mr. Heath's murder?"

"Honestly?"

My phone dings. I check my text.

This is Oliver. Keats sent me your number. Sorry, Rosi. Jade's in the bathroom, so I have to be quick. She WAS in the security closet but with me. We were fooling around. Before I met you for dinner. That's all though. Anyway, sorry I couldn't help. I know this project is important to you.

"Is everything okay?" Officer Daniel asks, reading the disgust in my face.

"Jade didn't kill Brent Heath," I say with exasperation. "She and Oliver were fooling around in there." I hold out my phone for him to read the text.

"Huh. Do you believe him?"

"I do. He and Keats are college buddies."

"Well, at least we can knock Andy and Jade off our list of possible suspects."

"And Oliver," I say. "You can knock Oliver off the list, too."

"That's a good day's work in my book," says Officer Daniel.

"If you say so."

Chapter 13

"Do you have any other theories?" Keaton spoons me from behind as we snuggle in his bed. Barley and I had decided to spend the night. Ruthie has been hiding under the bed. Poor kitty.

"I really don't. But we are losing money every day this project sits idle. Some of the machinery and tools that Jakob needs for the project are rented for a certain period of time. Every day the site is closed down, the more likely we'll need extensions with those things, and subcontractors might be busy with other projects. The plan had been built with precision, and now everything's been thrown off. Money. Money. Money."

"What about something more positive? Tell me about the mural project. Any submissions yet?"

"Oh my gosh, yes! There are some very talented people living in this retirement community. But I'm sworn to secrecy about the most competitive idea. Trust me that it's going to be amazing!"

"And cost saving."

"Yes, for sure. Jade's original idea for a hanging sculpture from the ceiling would have cost $5000! I still can't believe the board approved that idea!"

"Probably supported by Jan and Brenda."

Probably so," I laugh. "Oh! I forgot to tell you that Gabby sent pics from the contents of the box that Andy took."

"She had pictures?"

"Yeah, thank goodness she took them before he stole the box. Want to see?"

"Heck, yeah, I do!"

I sit up and pull my phone from the nightstand. Barley jumps on the bed and fills the space that's now opened between Keats and me. I scroll through my messages until I find the one from Gabby. "Here you go," I say, holding out my phone. "Old PBR bottles, a vintage key, a black cinder block, and a half of hundreds of $100 bills."

Keaton takes the phone and stares at the images. He pauses to use his fingers to enlarge one picture in particular, the black cinder block. "Rosi!" His eyes get large as he talks. "Rosi, I know this cinder block!"

"What?" I ask, confused.

"There is only one home in all of Tucson Valley that has this kind of black cinder block."

"What do you mean?"

"When you called me yesterday, do you remember me telling you that I was raking leaves at the old mansion that used to be part of the Tucson Valley Retirement Community?"

"The mansion is made of black cinder blocks?"

"The foundation is made from these bricks and an old shed on the property, too."

"What do you think it means?"

"I have no idea."

"Wait a minute!" Now it's my turn to get excited. "Do you think the other half of this money could be buried on the property?"

"Maybe? But even so, what's the connection between the site where the box was found and the mansion? It was old Roland Price's property where the box was found."

I shake my head back and forth. "No, you're wrong. The box was found buried in part of TVRC's original property, where the parking lot for the tech center is going to be added as soon as we get the go ahead from Officer Daniel to continue work."

"Interesting. But the two pieces of property are about as far away from each other as possible—bookending the original property."

"That's it!" I yell so loud that Barley jumps up and starts barking. "Both black cinder blocks represent the outer edges of the Tucson Valley Retirement Community property."

"Rosi, I know you have a proven track record when it comes to solving mysteries, but even if you are correct in your analysis, what's the purpose?"

"I don't know, but I'm going to talk to the people that live in that mansion." I get out of bed and throw on my old University of Illinois sweatshirt. "Wait! Are the owners nice? I've met my quota of tormenters the past few months."

"They are a young couple. With a lot of money. The wife is a software developer."

"Sounds like Simon."

"Yeah. And the husband's a lawyer. They have a couple of little kids."

"Okay. Sounds harmless enough. Do you think you could come with me to talk to them, since you already have a connection and so I don't sound like a madwoman when I show up asking about black cinder blocks and old PBRs?"

"What's your script when you talk to them?"

"I have no idea, but I'll let you know when I'm out of the shower!"

I put on a pair of khaki capris and a ¾ sleeved polka-dot red shirt. I look a bit like Minnie Mouse, but Minnie is harmless, and that is the look I am going for when I show up at a stranger's house and request to look around their property. No black, incognito clothing choices. I brush out my brown hair, which is in serious need of a trim, and carefully pull out two stray gray hairs. Even gray hair won't dampen my spirits today.

Keaton, dressed in blue jeans and a Bon Jovi t-shirt, looks casually chic and hot—*my* hot landscaper boyfriend. I'm so glad he's not working on this Saturday. We drop Barley off at my place first. She's not pleased to be cast aside, but I know she will be asleep in five minutes.

The mansion is much more impressive up close than viewed from the street as I had observed a few times, though not many, as technically the home no longer belongs within the limits of the retirement community. It certainly doesn't look anything like the other homes in Tucson Valley. A massive porch spans the front of the house with a circular bump-out forming a bubble-like room on the front left side. It reminds me of the shape of the room at the new tech center that will house the virtual reality technology. A giant stained glass window faces the massive yard filled with trees that remind me of the trees you'd find in the Midwest. No wonder Keaton's landscaping company had been hired to rake. The black cinder block foundation contrasts with the rest of the cinder block structure of the house that's been painted a crisp white color to give the home a more modern look. I wish for a tour inside, but that's even more presumptuous than asking the owners to let strangers look around the *outside* of their property. Keaton had texted the owner to explain why we were coming by.

A young man in his late 20s or early 30s is waiting for us on the front porch when we arrive. He wears a University of Arizona hoodie and black athletic shorts and Nike shoes. His curly hair has grown out, making his hair appear like a small shrub on his head which is the style in men's hair these days. Zak has done the same with his hair, and even though his hair is straight line mine and Wesley's, the sheer volume of it creates a large helmet of hair that he thinks makes him look more attractive. I won't be the one to tell him he needs a haircut as everyone else his age looks the same. The man waves at Keaton. He waves back, and I follow behind.

"Hello, Cody. Thanks for agreeing to meet with us." He and Keaton shake hands. "This is Rosi Laruee."

I reach my hand out, too. "Thanks so much. I know this may be a surprise to you."

"Keaton didn't tell me much, just something about a black cinder block from an old box that might match our house?"

The front door opens, and an attractive young woman walks out onto the porch. Her hair is pulled into a topknot, and she has a baby strapped to her chest in one of those wearable baby carriers. A toddler hides behind her legs. "Hello, welcome," she says warmly, extending her hand. "I'm Annabeth."

I take her hand and feel instantly calmed by her friendly smile. "We are so sorry to intrude. You obviously have your hands full with two littles ones." I wave at the little boy who peeks at me from behind his mom.

"Not at all. They're *easy* compared to the renovations we've been doing on this old house."

"When did you make the purchase?" Keaton asks.

"Six months ago, and don't let my wife fool you," says Cody. "We're pulling our hair out at times trying to manage these kiddos and this house at the same time. We are currently recovering from a sewage backup."

"That's no fun," I say. "Maybe we should come back at another time."

"No way. One of the main reasons we purchased this house is because we love the history that comes with a vintage home. Any chance that our property connects to whatever you found on the construction site is super exciting."

"Awesome!" My heart quickens with expectation as it matches Annabeth's excitement. "Can I show you some pictures of what was found in the box?"

"Yes, please!" The toddler detaches from his mother's leg and grabs a race car from a basket on the porch and rolls it back and forth, talking to himself as he plays.

I take out my phone and pull up the pictures that Gabby had forwarded me and pass it to Cody. "This is the image that drew Keaton to suggest looking for clues on your property." I show her the picture of the black cinder block.

"It sure looks like our foundation blocks. Let's take a closer look." We follow Cody down the front porch steps, including the little boy with his race car. Cody carries my phone to the side of the house where he drops to his knees. Several times he looks back and forth between the picture on my phone and the foundation of his house. "Yep, there. See that little indentation on this cinder block, kind of like the letter C."

Keaton, Annabeth, and I squat on the ground to look at the black cinder block. "I see it," says Annabeth.

"Now look at the picture."

We crowd around Cody to look at my phone. "It's the same marking," Keaton says.

My palms start to sweat just as they used to do when I'd be investigating a story for the Springfield Gazette and found a hot lead. "Scroll to the next pictures."

"Old beer bottles?" Cody asks, scrunching up his nose.

"Pabst Blue Ribbon is the brand," I say.

"My granddad used to drink that," says Keaton.

"So did someone that used to live here," says Cody, looking with surprise at all of us.

"What do you mean, hon?" asks Annabeth, adjusting the baby on her chest and checking to make sure her son is nearby.

"Do you remember when I cleaned out that old shed over there?" He points to a run-down shed on the edge of the property. The shingles on the roof have come off in a couple of places, and the window in the shed door is broken. The structure of the building looks solid, though, as the entire shed is built with black cinder blocks.

"It's the shed," I say, walking across the yard. "The whole thing is built with black cinder blocks!" My adrenaline flies through my veins with every step I take closer to the structure.

"Wait!" hollers Cody. "I didn't even get a chance to tell you about the beer bottles I found in there!"

"Can we get inside? Have you found a box? Like the one these items were found in?"

"Slow down, Rosi. Give the man a chance to think," says Keaton as he catches up with me.

I realize that I have been running all of my thoughts through my mind faster than doughnuts gliding down a conveyor belt at Krispy Kreme. "Sorry! I have a hunch that the other half of the money might be in the shed and…"

"Money?" Annabeth asks.

"Oh! Right! Advance the picture on my phone. A black cinder block brick and PBR bottles weren't all that was found on our construction site."

Cody moves to the next picture after I reenter my password. "A key?" Annabeth looks over his shoulder.

"A vintage key, yes. Now swipe one more time."

Cody stares at the screen, studying the halves of hundred dollar bills that are spread out in the box in the image. "Money?"

"Five thousand dollars. Well, one half of five thousand dollars."

"Twenty-five hundred dollars?" asks Annabeth.

"No, like a half of fifty $100 bills."

"So, the money is useless without the other halves," says Cody.

"And you think the other halves might be in our shed?" asks Annabeth. The baby starts to fuss, and she reapplies her pacifier.

I lift up my shoulders. "Maybe? I think the black cinder block is a pretty strong connection. And both your property and ours at the senior center are on complete opposite sides of the Tucson Valley Retirement Community."

"But our home isn't in the retirement community," says Cody.

"It used to be," says Keaton.

"Right! Remember, babe? When we closed on the house, the previous owner complained about the HOA board at the retirement community and warned us to stay away from some lady named Brenda if she came snooping around trying to get us to deed our land back to them—or at least part of it."

"Right! She told us that the board wanted to expand their property and that we should donate some of our land since we sit on two lots, that the founders would have wanted that because our home was in the original property lines of the retirement village."

"Well, don't worry about that happening. Some guy died on the other side of TVRC and left the property to us in the will."

"And that's where you are putting the technology center?" asks Annabeth.

"Exactly, but the box was found on our original property near the senior center. It had been buried in a grassy area that's been recently dug up to put in a parking lot for the tech center."

"I am so confused," says Annabeth.

"Me, too," says Keaton, running his hand through his hair.

"I think Rosi is on to something." We all look at Cody whose eyes begin to widen as if a lightbulb has been turned on in his mind. "Annabeth, remember that map we found in the wall we took down between the kitchen and the dining room, the one that had the poor patch work in the wall?"

"I remember," she says slowly.

"What kind of map?" I am getting excited again.

"Let me get it. Come on, CJ. Follow Mommy to the house."

The little boy named CJ skips behind his mom into the house.

"You've really brightened her spirits," Cody says quietly as soon as his wife is out of earshot.

"Oh?" I ask.

"Baby number two has been kicking our butts. This is a nice diversion. Thank you."

"Well, we haven't figured anything out yet, but it's fun to guess. I'm sorry about your rough days. I only had one child and barely made it through. But you will. I promise that you'll never regret your decision to have kids."

"How many children do you guys have?"

"Us? No, none," I say. Keaton smiles kindly as he waits for me to explain. "I have one child, a grown son, from a previous marriage."

"Gotcha. And no children from your second marriage?"

"Second marriage?" I look at Keaton as his smile grows bigger.

"No second marriage for either of us, at least not yet. I mean, maybe in the future. I mean, one of us might have a second marriage in the future. Or maybe both of us will have a second marriage. But not now. We don't…"

Annabeth returns to save me from myself. "Here you go. It took me a while. The house is kind of a mess." She looks sheepishly at her husband.

Cody takes the map from his wife and opens it up. It's a simple drawing written on what looks to be an old piece of paper from a spiral notebook like the kind we had in school, clearly not on paper from the early days of the home. On one side of the paper is a giant black X, and on the other side of the paper is a matching X. What look to be small rectangles are drawn next to each X. Hundred dollar bills?

"Even if this map proves there is a connection between your box and our property, how do we know where to look for the money?" asks Cody.

"Didn't you say you found old beer bottles in the shed when you cleaned it out?" asks Annabeth who is simultaneously patting her baby's arm and holding her toddler's hand.

Cody pauses before asking another question. "How many owners lived here prior to us?"

"This house sat empty for many years, but I imagine the property is from the 30s or 40s. The Tucson Valley Retirement Community opened sometime in the '80s. Your property's separation from TVRC happened at least five years ago. One of the guys on my landscaping crew told me about it when we were working on your yard," says Keaton. "Something about the last owner dying

145

shortly after he won the right to maintain the home outside of TVRC's limits, and he didn't have any children."

"That's sad," says Annabeth. She squeezes CJ's hand.

"My buddy told me the old man had quite a reputation as a real cutup. Everybody's grandpa kind of guy. He was well liked. His niece, who got the house in the old man's will, was going to fix the house up, but she got a job promotion and moved to Salt Lake City. She finally gave up the dream of living here herself. That's when she put it on the market. It's a shame the house has been empty for so long."

"Do you know when your house was built?" I ask.

"The deed said 1949."

"Wow! The house looks way older than that. Oops! I mean, you know what I'm saying, right? I'm sure it's gorgeous on the inside."

"It *will be* gorgeous on the inside when we're done renovating," Cody says, beaming with pride, "But we wanted a vintage house. We sure got it!"

My phone dings, and I realize that Cody is still holding it. He hands it back to me.

Need to talk to you in person ASAP.

"What's the matter?" Keaton asks, judging the concern on my face.

"Mario needs to see me soon. Very soon."

"Can you give me a minute before you leave? I have an idea," says Cody.

I nod my head. Cody enters a code on a lock on the dilapidated shed door. He pulls the lock free and hands it to his son to play with. "I found the beer bottles back here." He points to the corner of the shed under a rudimentary wooden slab that has been bolted to the back of the black cinder block wall to make a bench.

"The floor is dirt," I say with surprise. I wouldn't have expected that with how well-built the walls are constructed."

"I know. I always thought that was weird, too. This shed was a disaster. So much trash piled up. Old furniture, boxes of tools, rusty coffee cans, gardening supplies, Christmas decorations, and a whole lot of junk. I don't know if it had ever been cleared out before."

"And the beer bottles were in the corner?" asks Keaton.

"Yeah. I didn't find them for weeks after I began deconstructing the mess in here."

Keaton picks up a wooden yardstick that's hanging on the wall. "Do you mind?" he asks.

"Help yourself," says Annabeth.

We watch Keaton walk to the corner of the shed. He uses the yardstick to dig at the dirt in the corner under the bench. He digs for a few minutes, not getting more than six inches below the surface, when we hear a sound. Metal.

"He found it," says Annabeth. "He found it, CJ!"

"Yippee! Yippee!" CJ says over and over as he and his mother jump up and down, the baby bobbing along with her brother and mother.

I ignore another message from Mario.

Cody joins Keaton in the dirt, and together the two of them dig out the box. Looking identical to the box pictured on my phone, they set it on the bench. With the sun dipping behind the clouds, I turn on the spotlight of my phone and point it at the box.

"There's a spot for a key," says Cody. He looks at me as if I can solve this problem.

"You're not getting the key," I say. "Someone took the box who might not give it back without police involvement."

"What?" Annabeth and Cody ask at the same time.

"I'm sorry. I really don't have time to explain. I have a work emergency."

"Okay, then we need a solution."

"What about a piece of wire?" Annabeth asks, pointing to a box of garden supplies.

"Maybe."

Keaton grabs wires and begins twisting them into various widths. Cody takes each one and tries it in the keyhole of the box until finally—finally—the box opens.

"Holy shi—" says Cody before Annabeth throws her hands over CJ's ears.

"There's the rest of your money," I say.

"Yeah," says Cody. He rocks side to side on his feet breathing quickly.

"This is really cool, hon," says Annabeth, rubbing her hand along her husband's arm to calm him.

"Yeah," he repeats.

"I can't believe I have to leave *now*, but I do. I'm really sorry. I know we've only met, but please trust me that

I'm going to do everything I can to get you the other half of that money. Keaton has your number. I promise to call tonight. It was so nice meeting your lovely family!"

I drag Keaton by the hand out of the shed and across the yard feeling the pull from one adrenaline fueled experience to another. Someday I might have a quiet day in Tucson Valley. But not today.

Chapter 14

I'm too rattled to drive, so Keaton starts my car for our drive to the senior center. It's so unusual for Mario to be working at the senior center on a Saturday when there is no performance scheduled.

"What's Mario been texting that has you so anxious?" asks Keaton.

"I don't know what's going on, but Mario isn't one for overconcern. If he says he needs to see me right away then it's important."

"Okay. Do you want me to stay behind while you talk to him?"

I look at Keaton with both shock and admiration. "Do you honestly think that I'd keep secrets from you at this point in our relationship?" He puts his hand on my knee and keeps it there the rest of the way to the senior center.

Come to the security closet.

"What's it say?"

"He's waiting in the security closet."

When we arrive, Mario is pointing to the monitor in the security closet, and Tracy is staring at the screen through her reading glasses. I hadn't expected to see her, too.

"Oh no! Oh! Oh!" She looks away from the screen, clutching her chest. When she turns around to acknowledge me, her pupils are as big as rolls of masking tape. She points at the screen.

"Hi, Rosi. Thanks for coming." Mario rewinds the footage and steps aside for Keaton to move closer to the screen, too. He starts the video again. At first, nothing happens. There are no people in the range of the camera. Then I see Brent Heath walk onto the site. He's adjusting his tool belt on his waist as he walks toward the front of the tech center. He carries a can of paint that he sets next to the building.

"Who's that?" asks Keaton as he points to someone walking into view of the camera.

"It's Jakob. It's Jakob Beacher." I put my hand over my chest to will by heart to calm down, but it doesn't work.

Jakob walks toward Brent. The men engage in conversation that grows more heated with lots of finger pointing including at the can of yellow paint that sits on the ground. At one point Brent gets close to Jakob's face and pushes him in the chest. Jakob backs up, almost tripping over the paint can. More yelling. More shoving—this time from Jakob, too. And then it goes awry, from bad to worse in mere seconds. Jakob reaches for Brent's tool belt, catching Brent off guard and causing him to stumble, the building catching his fall. Jakob grabs Brent's nail gun and fires the fatal blows into Brent's chest that drop him to the ground by the front door. He runs away with the nail gun, and Mario turns off the footage.

"I thought the camera was turned off," Keaton says, his face a mixture of red and green, like he might be seconds away from vomiting.

"So did we," says Mario. Keaton cocks his head and looks at him in confusion.

"You followed up with the security company?" I ask, remembering my conversation with Mario.

"I did. I called them and spoke with a very helpful tech support woman who walked me through the steps that pulled the footage from some place called the cloud." He takes a quick deep breath. "Can you imagine such a delightful place like a cotton candy puff cloud holding onto a murder?"

I give a small smile. It's not the time to chastise my co-workers about the need to update their knowledge of technology. They will learn all about the wonders of modern technology soon enough when the tech center opens.

"The footage was erased, Rosi. Jakob erased the footage. Can you believe it?"

I hang my head, shocked by this unexpected discovery. "I never would have pegged Jakob for a murderer. I guess Brent went too far with whatever he was saying to him."

"A man can only take so much," Mario says quietly. He looks up into our surprised faces. "Not that I condone murder!" He holds his hands up as if to say, *I'm not guilty of anything.*

"Have you shown Officer Daniel?" I ask.

"Not yet. I wanted you to see it first," says Mario. "You and Tracy. And Keaton."

"I'll call him."

Tracy leans against the wall with her eyes closed. "Are you okay?" I ask, gently touching her arm.

"Rosi, they looked like they were fighting over paint color. Paint color!"

"Maybe," I say, but we don't know for sure.

"Our choice of yellow paint color for the outside of the building led to murder."

"Don't be silly, Tracy," says Mario. "You had no role in Jakob's choices to pull out Brent's nail gun and use it as a weapon."

"Of course not," Keaton agrees.

But I can't say anything because I'm not sure she's wrong.

Chapter 15

Things in the Tucson Valley Retirement Community haven't gotten any less crazy since Jakob's arrest for Brent Heath's murder, but the crazy now isn't murderous rage crazy brought on by one too many put downs from the construction manager. Instead, the crazy is caused by the impending opening of the Roland Price Technology Center, a shining light for all other retirement communities across the nation, reminding us all of the value in investing in technology for *all* ages, not just the young.

Jakob hadn't gone down without a fight, according to Officer Daniel. He'd been found hiding underneath one of his twin's beds after hours of searching for him. When he was finally put into cuffs, he'd started trying to twist the story that he'd been acting in self-defense, but as the tape clearly showed, choosing to pierce someone's heart with a nail gun isn't exactly equal payback for getting yelled at by the boss.

In the three weeks since Jakob's arrest, so much has happened, but one of my favorite unexpected joys was finding out that the board had voted on Karen's mural proposal for the new entry wall in the tech center. Friday, at the ribbon cutting ceremony, the mural will be revealed. It's a real beauty as I had the pleasure of watching her paint over the last week. People will be so surprised that the quiet, mousy, understated woman created such an amusing and interesting recognition of all that encompasses Tucson Valley. Watching her boyfriend Bob Horace delivering food as she worked reminded me of the beauty of love, and for the first time, I allowed myself to think long term about my relationship with Keaton.

"Come in!" I say when someone knocks on my office door. "Hello, Officer Daniel," I say, smiling. "This is an unexpected visit." Dan is wearing jeans and a white polo shirt. His thinning hair is combed nicely to cover as much of his growing hairline as possible. "No uniform today?"

"Not today," he says. "It's fall break in the school district, and I'm using one of my personal days. Caliope and I are driving up to Tucson for a little hiking in the Saguaro National Park."

"Oh! I take it your first couple of dates went well."

"You could say that," he smiles sheepishly. "I wanted to thank you for getting the ball rolling, so to speak. If you hadn't told me about Caliope talking about me during book club, I never would have had the guts to ask her out.

I don't tell him that I waited for that information reveal because I was mad at him for making fun of my theory that Andy may have been responsible for Brent's murder. "I really am happy for the two of you. Remember to be kind, Dan. No arrogant moves. Teachers don't like attitudes. They have to deal with that enough each day with their students."

"Yeah, she's shared some crazy stories. I promise I am being on my best behavior. I also came by to tell you that Andy has finally been apprehended and charged with theft for taking the box that he and Gabby found buried in the construction site."

"Where was he found?"

"New Mexico. He'd fled to his brother's place and is being extradited back to Arizona as we speak."

"I really hope that the money in the box is returned to Cody and Annabeth. They deserve it."

"But half of the money was found on the senior center property, too, Rosi. You could make a claim for $2500 on behalf of the retirement community."

"I know. Could you do me a favor?"

"Maybe."

"Can you keep this box information between Tracy, you, and me? I don't think the board members need to share their opinions. If Tracy and I want that sweet young family to get all of the $5000, then I think the decision shouldn't be complicated with the opinions of people like Brenda Riker and Jan Jinkins."

"I can definitely agree to that secret."

"Will you be at the ribbon cutting ceremony on Friday?" I ask before Officer Daniel leaves.

"You better believe it. The middle school students are singing the national anthem, so, uh, Caliope will be there, too."

"I look forward to seeing you both. Have fun on your hike. And be careful on those rocks. They can be slippery! I've learned that the hard way."

I walk outside with Barley on her leash to check on Keaton and his team's last touches with the landscaping around the sidewalks and in front of the Roland Price Technology Center. The gorgeous orange flowers of the cape honeysuckle shrubs compliment the beautifully painted building, paying homage to the brilliant Arizona sunlight and the optimism that this project promises. The choice in paint color wasn't worth a man's life, but I'm still proud of the finished product. Along the outside of the virtual reality bump out of the building are a curved row of golden barrel cactus plants and metal statues created by the local high school using 3D technology in class.

Barley finds Keaton first, greeting him with a lick on the back of his neck as he's bent over a pot of red geraniums. "Hey there, Barley. Good to you, too." Keaton stands up and wipes the dirt from his hands onto his pants. "Hey, cutie." He grabs me with one hand around my waist and pulls me in for a kiss.

"Keaton! Aren't you worried that your crew will tease you?" I whisper into his ear.

"No way. I'll prove my confidence to you." He dips me back toward the ground where he bends down to kiss me again—until Barley licks me across the forehead almost causing Keaton to drop me. "Oops! I didn't figure in the interference of a fifty-pound beast. I think she might need another obedience class."

He laughs, and I join in. "Truth." My eyes wander to the spot in the sidewalk just in front of the main door where Barley's paw prints have made a lasting imprint in the concrete. That hadn't been my finest day as a dog mama when I lost control of Barley once again and long enough for her to traipse through the newly laid cement. Yet, nothing matters anymore when I am with Keaton. "Everything looks amazing out here," I say. "I can't wait for everyone in the community to see it on Friday."

"Thanks. I think the team outdid themselves."

"Hey, Rosi!" Gabby walks across the sidewalk toward Keaton and me. "This place rocks!" She plays an imaginary air guitar. "Hi, Barley. What a good dog you are!"

"Yeah, it's finally come together. Did you hear that the police found Andy?"

"Heck yeah I did. Not only is he going to jail for theft from the senior center, but I filed a complaint against him for theft, too."

"For the theft of something from you that he's already charged with theft for taking from someone else?" Keaton asks, scratching his head.

"Don't get hung up on the details, Keaton."

"I'm sure the police will sort it all out," I say, rolling my eyes and shaking my head behind Gabby's back. "What brings you by today? The unveiling isn't scheduled until Friday."

"I know, but seeing as both the general contractor and construction manager are otherwise *engaged,* I wondered if you and Tracy needed help with anything."

"That's really nice, Gabby. I think we're good. Jade's installing the final touches with furnishings inside right now. Maybe she could use some help if you're willing."

"Jade? No way," Gabby waves her pointer finger back and forth demonstrably. "I don't think she'd like *my* help," she smiles coyly.

"Why's that?" asks Keaton.

"Rosi, do you remember when that hot architect came up as a topic of conversation at book club?"

"I remember," I say, batting my eyes at Keaton who just shakes his head. "You called him a meathead."

"Yeah, well, anyway, he's stayed in town to finish things up, to kind of be the de facto leader."

"Yes, Oliver has been a big help."

"Well, he's not only helping the retirement community. Let's just say he's helped get me out of my dating slump, too. And I don't think Ms. Jade would appreciate that fact." She throws her head back in hysterical laughter.

"Oliver's making the rounds—" Keaton says, before stopping when I poke him in the side.

"You have fun, Gabby. See you on Friday?"

"I wouldn't miss it. Oh, one more thing!"

"Yes?"

"I found my nail gun. I know that it was Brent's own nail gun that killed him. I've seen the news reports, but I was still perplexed about what happened to mine."

"And?"

"It was found in a wheelbarrow of stuff that was cleared out of the site by the police when they were collecting evidence. I guess I'd left it on the job." She shrugs her shoulders. "It happens. Anyway, see you guys on Friday!"

"She's a ball of energy," Keaton says after Gabby walks away.

"As is Oliver."

"As is Oliver."

Chapter 16

The morning of the ribbon cutting ceremony is busy, busy, busy. Ross from the construction crew is helping Mario set up folding chairs for any of the guests that want to sit. Tracy is reattaching the canvas over the mural that fell down last night. No sneak peeks allowed. I am looking over the program to make sure I didn't forget anything.

"Rosi?"

I look up from my desk to see Cody and Annabeth Corum. This time the baby is attached around the front of Cody, and Annabeth is holding CJ in her arms. "Hello! What a nice surprise. Are you here for the ribbon cutting ceremony?" I look at the clock on the wall behind them. "You're a little bit early, but feel free to walk the grounds. The landscaping is exceptionally beautiful."

"No," says Annabeth. "We can't make the ceremony. It's during naptime."

"Ah, yes. I remember those days. Sacred part of the day."

Annabeth smiles. "We wanted to give you something, Rosi—for the big day. Can you come with us?"

"Oh, okay." I'm glad I left Barley home today. There is much too much excitement in the air. I follow the Corum family out of my office and down the hall to the back door.

"It's in our truck," Cody says.

We stop outside their pickup truck. The black asphalt is absorbing the sun's rays, but the temperature is so mild at 75 degrees, that it feels wonderful to be standing outside in the middle of a parking lot.

Cody opens the tailgate of the pickup. A large tarp covers something in the truck bed. "After your visit and the subsequent discovery of the money, Cody and I began to wonder if there might be other clues or treasures with hidden meaning on the property. We instantly remembered a large statue that we found in a back room in the basement. I'm assuming that the previous owners didn't venture in that basement much more than we had. It's a dirty, spider web-covered, dark place."

"What kind of statue?"

"Let me tell you more first," says Cody. "We started investigating in that part of the basement to see if anything stood out that we'd missed before."

"And we found something," says Annabeth softly.

"We found a small piece of paper, wrapped up like a scroll and tied with twine, resting in the hand of the statue."

I want to ask all the questions but instead I clasp my hands together and squeeze them tightly to keep from blurting them out.

Cody reaches into the truck bed and pulls out a small piece of paper, thin from age. He hands it to me. Read it."

I open the paper carefully and read aloud.

They say living is for the youth
That the aged get in the way
But they are missing the full truth
That life begins anew each day
For comes with age
Is wisdom due
You must engage
And start anew
Each day you wake
Find the joy around
Good choices make
And fun abounds
Don't fret the small stuff

Find good in all
You're good enough
So have a ball!

"That's really sweet. I'm not sure what it means, though," I say, handing the paper back to Cody.

"I think that the guy that wrote this poem—most likely the same old guy that buried the box—was saying that we should live life to the fullest no matter if we are young or old and to have fun along the way."

"Huh," I say, contemplating the deeper meaning of the words. "You might be right."

"Rosi, this statue has two arms spread wide with hands pointing in opposite directions. On the back of the property near the shed, there's an old concrete platform in the ground. I think the statue stood on that platform and pointed from our home to your senior center. For whatever reason, he wanted to create a treasure hunt for either the future owners of his home or the owners of the property where the senior center was built."

"Connecting the old with the new?" I ask, more to myself than to Annabeth and Cody. "The old is your home, and the new is the technology center. And, I guess, even the development of the retirement community itself, was new."

"There might be some truth in that theory, or it might just be a bored, old man planting a fun clue with a discarded statue on his property, but whatever the reason, we'd like to gift this statue to the Roland Price Technology Center. We've had the statue attached to a new base. We only ask that the hands continue to point in the directions of our home and the tech center, as I believe he would have intended."

"That's lovely. I think we can accommodate these wishes. Can I see the statue now?"

Annabeth pulls the tarp off the statue revealing a beautiful angel with outstretched wings and dainty hands pointing in opposite directions. Her weathered stone still shows the details of her simple frock and curly locks of hair. "She's beautiful. Stunning."

"We hoped you would say that," says Cody. "We used some of the money from the box to pay for the base—after the police returned it to us and we took it to the bank," says Cody.

"We thought it was the fair thing to do since Tracy insisted we keep the money," says Annabeth.

I feel the tears well up in my eyes, but they are happy tears. "It's lovely. All of this. Do you think I could get a plaque made with that poem to attach to the base?" I ask.

Annabeth smiles widely. "It's already there—on the other side."

I climb into the back of the truck to view the plaque on its side. "I can't imagine anything more perfect for today's celebration than unveiling this statue. Thank you."

"Ready?" asks Tracy as we prepare to walk out the back door of the senior center and into the common outdoor area that connects our building with the new technology center. She wears a teal skirt with a silky white top. Her wild curls are tamed with two yellow barrettes, a nod to our paint choice.

"I am ready—ready to introduce the tech center to the retirement community residents and ready to be *done* with this monstrous headache."

"Truth, sister. Truth."

I wipe away imaginary wrinkles from my flower print dress, take a deep breath, and push the door open. The chairs Ross and Mario had arranged are full. People stand two people deep behind the back row. I guess I under planned the attendance. A reporter from local station KVOA waves at me as we make our way to the podium in front of the chairs. I'd answered her questions ahead of time, including an early reveal of Karen as the winner of the mural competition which she'd agreed to keep quiet until after today's ceremony. I'd appreciated her thoughtfulness as a reporter, and it made me wistful for my days as a newspaper reporter in Illinois. Life has changed a lot in the last year.

Since Brent Heath is *unavailable,* and Jakob Heath is incarcerated, Oliver and Jade will be talking about the details of the project. I'm still not keen on their dalliances, but they are both grown adults, so what's it matter to me really? Plus, it seems Oliver has moved on to Gabby now.

I smile at Keaton who sits in the second row as I take my seat on stage next to Tracy who sits next to Jade. Oliver and Mayor Leo sit on the other side of the lectern. I look out over the crowd of people, so many faces having become familiar over the past months: Sweet Bob Horace, the owner of Barley's mother, and his new love interest, Karen, with the docile manners and easy smile. My new friends from book club: Helena, who'd provided baked goods for the reception after the ceremony, Gabby, who'd not only been a pivotal part of the construction of the Roland Price Technology Center, but also a fun person to be around, and Caliope, the newly dating partner of Officer Dan Daniel. From my vantage point, I think I can see their hands clasped between them. Even Jan and Brenda, for all of their personality shortcomings, have become an integral part of my world. If anything, they remind me how much I *don't* want to let myself become a crabby old lady when it's my time to own or rent a home in Tucson Valley. I can't wait for my parents to return soon to Arizona.

Mayor Leo Lestman walks to the lectern. "Ladies and gentlemen, thank you all for coming today. It is with great pride that I open the ceremonies for the dedication of the Roland Price Technology Center. This project started as a vision of Mr. Roland Price," he says, pointing to Danielle, his daughter-in-law. "With the generous donation of his property after his passing, Ms. Tracy Lake and the Tucson Valley Retirement Community Board put Mr. Price's vision into a plan that has grown into a project of epic proportions that will not only provide for a *building* for Tucson Valley's residents to engage with technology, but also a state-of-the-art location for technology to be harnessed for the improvement in quality of life socially, economically, creatively, and mentally, and in ways not yet imagined."

The audience applauds. Tracy talks next, highlighting the tech center's timeline in development, wisely skipping over the brief shutdown and murder of the construction manager by the general contractor. Oliver, looking especially dapper in a full suit and tie, talks about the architecture of the building and emphasizes some of the tech center's unique features like the virtual reality room. Jade talks about her décor choices including the use of furniture to make the population of Tucson Valley more comfortable with any special physical needs they may have. I look at Brenda who refuses to acknowledge that she is part of that demographic. She wears a predictable scowl on her face, though Jan seems more content. At least she is smiling. Of course, she's still sitting with her husband, and Brenda's husband is sitting three rows back.

"And Ms. Laruee will now unveil the winner of our mural competition," Jade says with little enthusiasm, still bent out of shape about not getting to design the entryway art.

"Hello, everyone! Thank you so much for joining us today to reveal this treasure in Southwestern Arizona that will be emulated by many for years to come. There are so many people that have pulled together as a team to leave their mark on this project, including my very naughty dog Barley. If you look closely by the front door you'll see her paw prints in the sidewalk." The crowd laughs. "That was *not* supposed to happen." They laugh again. "In addition to having the honor to reveal the artwork in the entryway of the tech center, another special treat arrived this morning that has just been installed thanks to my helpful elves Keaton, Mario, and Gabby. I'd like you to turn your attention to the covered statue in the grass area between the sidewalks connecting the senior center with the technology center." All eyes shift to the area where Mario stands. "Thanks to clues from a buried treasure—a puzzle of sorts—that was unveiled upon digging in this construction site, a unique connection was recently formed between the senior center and Cody and Annabeth Corum, owners of the large home on Wood Street. For those of you unfamiliar with the history of the Tucson Valley Retirement Community, that home at one time fell within our community limits. Thanks to the sense of humor of a previous owner and the generosity of the current owners, this uncovered treasure of sorts led to the discovery of this beautiful statue." I nod at Mario who pulls off the large burlap bag that covers the statue. We are all treated to the oohs and aahs of the audience. "The angel points with outstretched arms to the farthest ends of our community, arms opened wide to the possibilities found here. We hope you will stop and read the statue's inscription that was left by its original owner as well. We believe it encapsulates our hopes and wishes for Tucson Valley."

I turn my attention to Karen who sits in the front row next to Bob. She is wearing a simple black skirt and red top. Her hair sits in a bun at the nape of her neck making her look much older than her years, the perfect model for everyone's favorite grandma. "Now I would like to reveal the winner of our mural contest. What a treat to tell you about the extraordinary painting that awaits your viewing pleasure soon. Ms. Karen Parot, can you come to the stage, please?"

Bob stands and escorts Karen to the stage, holding her hand gently until she has walked up the two steps on the platform. Karen has already warned me that she would not speak, but she'd agreed to come on stage. "Karen Parot has been a resident of Tucson Valley for three years, moving here full time a year ago. Her vision for the mural was the inclusivity of its members which she highlights with skill and humor in the mural. She's titled it: *All People. All Personalities. All Moods. All Welcome. All the Time.* Please join me in congratulating Ms. Karen Parot."

"Woo Hoo! Karen! Yeah!" Bob's voice is the loudest. He stands up to help Karen off the stage and safely back to her seat after the applause has ended. Her face is beat red, but she is beaming.

"Thank you all for coming today. It's been an absolute pleasure to…"

"Awwwwww! Eek! Help! Help!"

I watch the crowd turn toward Brenda, who, in her skintight pleather green dress, stands on her folding chair screaming.

"Snake!" Jan jumps up from her seat, backing into Brenda's chair which collapses, sending Brenda sprawling onto the poor old man next to her. Everything happens so quickly, people standing up, half running toward the senior center and half running toward the tech center.

"I've got it!" Gabby runs toward the chaos, not away. With one fluid motion, she reaches down and picks up the back of the snake, enclosing it in the burlap bag that had covered the statue. She marches it away from the crowd and deposits the sack and the snake into a garbage can set up for the reception. "I told you we might see that critter again," Gabby says, proudly waving her hands at me.

I smile, looking out over the crowd of people: *All People. All Personalities. All Moods. All Welcome. All the Time.*

"Anyone up for a virtual reality African safari trip?" asks Tracy.

There's a mad rush to the front door of the Roland Price Technology Center.

"You're not going to get in line?" asks Keaton, as he joins me on the sidewalk next to his beautiful flowers.

"Me? No. I don't need to take a trip. I'm exactly where I want to be. Here. In the Tucson Valley Retirement Community. With you. And all of these quirky people." He squeezes my hand, the perfect ending to our opening ceremony, even if Brenda *did* win the battle that kept Bob from smashing a champagne bottle into the building. *Perhaps she needed that good luck with the snake and all,* I think, smiling slyly.

The Tucson Valley Retirement Community Cozy Mystery Series:

Dying to Go (Nothing to Gush About)

Thirty-nine-year-old Rosi Laruee—named Rosisophia Doroche after her mother's beloved Golden Girls—decides that the end of her twenty-year marriage and her dad's impending knee replacement surgery are all the excuses she needs to visit Tucson Valley Retirement Community. But the drama follows Rosi when she finds the body of local tart and business owner, Salem Mansfield. The information she discovers using her newspaper reporter sleuthing skills coupled with the clues she picks up from lackluster Police Officer Dan Daniel lead to a surprise discovery when the murderer is revealed. Along the way, she meets a cast of characters in her parents' social circle who leave her questioning her parents' choices in friends while simultaneously befriending many of the residents, including a handsome landscaper and a brand-new Golden Retriever puppy she names Barley. Rosi's visit to Tucson Valley proves more than she'd bargained for, but maybe, she realizes, it's just the kind of change she needs. Laugh out loud with Rosi, and be prepared to get the happy feels along the way!

Dying For Wine (Seeing Red)

There's a rockin' concert of 1960s impersonators coming to Tucson Valley to perform in the snowbird send-off concert at the Tucson Valley Retirement Community Performing Arts Center. And as the one in charge, Rosi Laruee is thriving in the chaos. Diva attitudes, outrageous requests, and late flights don't sideline what is meant to be the greatest concert this community has ever seen. That is, until a dead body shows up below the stage next to the front row of seats. Now, she's sleuthing again with Officer Dan Daniel. Only this time, the murder is personal, and she needs to restore the reputation of Tucson Valley as being a safe place by solving this mystery quickly. What she discovers is a much deeper web of connections than she could have imagined. Throw in a condo search, a budding relationship with Keaton, and a growing Golden Retriever to Rosi's crazy adventures, and you have a recipe for hours of laughter.

Dying For Dirt (All Soaped Up)

It's conference time, and Rosi and her co-workers are headed to the Senior Living Retirement Community Conference in Phoenix. But don't think that it's time off! Joined by some of the most delightful and most annoying representatives of Tucson Valley Retirement Community, the trip almost ends before it begins along Interstate 10. Things don't get easier when, at the opening ceremonies, Rosi makes a most unfortunate introduction of herself. When her golden retriever puppy discovers a dead body that same night, Rosi pivots to sleuthing again as hilarity follows her every move.

Dying to Build (Nailed It)

Tucson Valley is weeks away from unveiling the new Roland Price Technology Center which will make them the envy of all retirement communities in the country. But just as things are coming together, a key crew member is found dead at the construction site, throwing an unwanted spotlight on the trials and tribulations that seem to follow Rosi Laruee as she discovers another dead body yet again. Up against the clock and the pocketbook, will the murder be solved in time for the scheduled opening ceremony?

Dying to Dance (Cha-Cha-Ahhh) April 2024

The Secret of Blue Lake (1)

The only true certainty in life is dying, but there's a whole lot of life to live from beginning to end if you're lucky. When Chicago news reporter Meg Popkin's dad makes a surprise move to a tiny town called Blue Lake, Michigan, in the middle of nowhere and away from his family after losing his wife to cancer, she wonders if there is more to the move than *just a change of scenery*. With the help of a new, self-confident reporter at the station, Brian Welter, she tries to figure out what the secret attraction to Blue Lake is for its many new residents and along the way discovers that maybe she's been missing out on some of the joys of living herself.

Drama, mystery, and romance abound for Meg as she learns about love, loss, and herself.

The Secret of Silver Beach (2)

After solving the mystery of the secret of Blue Lake, Meg returns to Chicago and to her new job as co-host on Chicago Midday. But when poor chemistry with Trenton Dealy leads to problems on the show, Meg is assigned a travel segment that will send her on location all around Lake Michigan visiting beach towns and local tourist attractions. The trip takes her away from fiancé Brian who has to continue anchoring the nightly news in Chicago. When odd threats start hurtling in Meg's direction, she finally confesses to Brian and those closest to her that she might have a stalker. Do the threats have something to do with the new information she learned about her dad's past in the little town of St. Joseph, Michigan, or is there something bigger at play that threatens more than Meg's livelihood?

The Secret of Blue Lake:

Chapter 1

"There's a pile up on the Dan Ryan," says my boss Jerry Stanley, his excitement for the craziest of news stories on full display. "A milk tanker collided with a truck carrying cocoa powder." He laughs, a deep hearty laugh that fills the newsroom. "I can't make this stuff up."

"Headlines writing themselves, huh?" I shake my head. It's never a dull moment at WDOU.

"Chocolate Milk Causes Road Closure on Busy Chicago Interstate," he says, smiling.

"Take a crew and talk to some people if you can—witnesses and drivers."

"Are there any fatalities?" It's the worst part of my job. Covering deaths is never easy, but since Mom died it's nearly impossible.

"No fatalities, Meg." He pats me on the shoulder. "Now get going. Take Brian with you. He needs to learn his way around Chicago," says Jerry.

I roll my eyes. The last thing I want to do is take our newest reporter Brian Welter *anywhere*. Before I can protest, I feel Brian's presence, his stale hidden-but-not-hidden cigarette stench permeating from his suit jacket. "Meggin Popkin!" He slaps the wall outside Jerry's office. "I hear I'm hanging with the number one street reporter."

I groan. No one calls me *Meggin* anymore. In a world full of Jennifers, Michelles, and Kristis, my parents bucked the trend and named their second child Megan, a different but regular-enough sounding name that they spelled M-E-G-G-I-N. I can appreciate their quest for originality, but with everyone spelling my name wrong, it was simpler to call myself Meg.

"Earth to Meggin!" Brian shouts through his cupped hands. No one should be allowed to yell at another person so closely unless in the throes of passion.

I wince at the sound of his annoying voice, ignore him, and head to my cubicle. He follows, landing in step with me. The news station abounds with energy and business, always with something going on in the Chicagoland area: the sounds of fingers on keys punching out stories or answering emails, the police scanners blaring, waiting to point a reporter to a new crime to cover, and the faint sound of elevator music playing through the overhead speakers that aim to calm the anxieties of the stories covered here.

"I'll meet you by the station van," I say. "I need to grab my phone."

"It's okay. I can wait for you. We can share an elevator. Go ahead and fix your hair, too, of course."

I know he's smiling a nauseating grin without even seeing his face. I've met this kind. I almost married this kind once before when I was young and dumb. Now I know better. But I don't get asked my opinion about new on-air talent. Even though Brian Welter comes with accolades galore for his on-air presence in Tucson, his *in-person* presence is nothing short of arrogance.

I ignore Brian as I grab my jacket along with my phone while shutting down my laptop. I have a superstition about leaving my computer on when I'm not at my desk. I don't want anyone seeing a story before it's buffed up and ready for its audience.

Brian stands to the side of the hallway as I brush past him. He rushes by to push the elevator button like a little boy fighting with his sister over who gets to push all the buttons. When Lara and I were little, we'd been assigned days. I got to do the "things" on even-numbered days while Lara got to do them on the odd-numbered days. Mom said that system cut our arguments in half. Something tells me Brian was an only child who never learned the value of compromising or perhaps the oldest who always thinks he's right. I can't help but glance in the elevator mirror before the door opens, making sure my bangs are aligned and no strands of my shoulder-length brown hair have parted on their own accord. Satisfied, I slide out the door before Brian.

Brian reaches the station van first and grabs the passenger seat door handle before I can stop him.

"No, you don't," I say, slapping my hand on the door handle, too.

"There's not room for both of us, kid." He brushes my hand away as he slips into the van.

"What an ass." I slam the backseat door.

"You'd better not mess with Meg, man," says Tom. We make eye contact through the rearview mirror. You don't make friends at a news station by ruffling the feathers of the cameraman.

"Her? I think I can handle *Meggin*," he says, laughing.

"I don't need *handling*. Drive, Tom." Tom accelerates so quickly that Brian's phone slides off the dashboard and crashes into the door.

"Dammit, Tom!" he says as he reaches for his phone.

Tom, our cameraman, has been recording my news segments since I first came to WDOU five years ago. Tom and I are more than work associates. We are friends. He and his wife, Anita, were the first people in line at Mom's visitation when she died. He still brings me leftovers once a week, either extra meat he'd grilled with a side of potatoes or an extra portion of stir fry. Tom cares for me like a little sister. I know he's got my back.

I put in my AirPods before I can hear more of Brian's drivel. I watch the busy city streets pass by as we race to the scene of the chocolate milk interstate. It's easy to imagine myself living on one of those little side streets living the life of a school librarian like I'd grown up thinking I'd be. Walking the stacks, looking for the perfect alphabetical placement, sneaking in readings of newly published books. There are days when I wished I'd never gone with Dad to his job at the newspaper, when management had called for a reporter to cover the local school board meeting, and he'd looked at me and asked his boss to let me go because no one wanted the gig. And I'd gone. And I'd fallen in love with telling stories, stories of boring school board meetings to stories of convenience store break-ins to stories of interstate pileups. But some days I still wonder what it would be like living the privacy of a librarian's job without being critiqued for every outfit choice or inadvertent nose booger.

Tom grabs his camera after finally finding a place to park in a back alley between Garfield and S. Wentworth Avenue. We take the chance of getting towed, and it wouldn't be the first time. The station budgets for such expenses. *Get to the story first. Worry about the van second.*

It's a hike up the embankment to the interstate. No one should get twenty feet within distance of a Chicago interstate under normal circumstances, the cars flying miles over the speed limit, weaving in and out of traffic. But no one is moving today. I count fifteen cars that have experienced some bit of fender or bumper damage, the highway beneath our feet a cloudy brown color mixing the cocoa powder from one over-turned semi-trailer with the milk of another. I toss a glance at the side streets below the interstate and wonder again why I'm not living the life of a single librarian. It might not seem glamorous, but to me it sounds perfect right about now. The early spring temperatures in Chicago make me shiver involuntarily. I hope the chocolate milk washes away the dirty snow that lines the road. Only the first winter snow in Chicago is welcome. Every snow after lingers as a mess of dirt and trash and pollution alongside the streets for months until the temperatures warm up long enough for fresh rains to wash it away.

"Meg, you have a perspective yet?" asks Tom. He rests a camera on his shoulder and points at the scene before us, a mess of banged up-cars and trucks with people on their phones and milling around the scene talking with police and other emergency workers.

"Yeah, sorry. I'll start with that blue car. It's the closest one to the cocoa powder truck." I point to a large white truck with pictures of chocolate bars on the side. I remember that I haven't eaten lunch today. The truck is on its side, the back half blocking the right lane of traffic and the back door swung open with punctured containers of cocoa powder spilling out. The milk truck it collided with is also on its side, in the adjoining left lane with its back door open, too. Milk continues to drip down and out the truck and into the cocoa powder below.

Tom starts to follow me as I weave between cars heading to the young woman who is leaning against her car and talking on the phone. Her compact car rests against the side of the road with a bumper that looks like a large accordion after making what looks like impact with the back tire of the cocoa powder truck.

I flash my station credentials in front of her. She drops the phone to her side.

"Excuse me, miss. I'm Meg Popkin with WDOU. I'd like to ask you a few questions."

She looks at Tom who is directing his camera at her. "Okay. I can talk," she says, brushing her hands through her long brown hair, a not-so-subtle attempt to be camera ready. "I...I've been crying," she says as she looks at the camera.

I smile reassuringly. "I imagine you have. It's been a scary day."

She smiles, too, comforted by the first in-person contact she's had since the accident. "I'm Quinn," she says.

Quinn answers my questions, becoming visibly calmer as I finish learning about the accident and its effect on her. She'd been talking to her boyfriend on the phone—hands free, of course—when the collision had occurred from behind, sending her sliding into the back of the semi-truck. She's relaxed enough to laugh about the absurdity of the mess that covers the interstate. "I guess all we need now are some cookies," she says amused with her own wit.

I thank her for her time and turn to leave when Brian grabs the microphone from my hand. I hadn't even noticed he was standing behind me. "What the...?" I ask.

"Quinn, when will you be filing your lawsuit?" he asks, thrusting the microphone so close to Quinn's face it nearly knocks out a tooth.

"A what?" She wrinkles her nose and looks at me.

"Give me back my microphone," I say, trying to yank it from Brian's firm grip.

He pulls it away and back into Quinn's face. "A lawsuit," he repeats. "You stand to make a lot of money from this accident, you know?"

"I...I don't want money. I want my car fixed and to move on. This has been the scariest day of my life." She looks at me, any sense of calmness disappearing from her face.

"Shut off the camera," I say to Tom. He glances at Brian who is giving him a stink eye while shaking his head back and forth. "Shut it off, Tom," I repeat.

Tom nods his head and pulls the camera from his shoulder. He knows who the boss is here. "Thanks, Quinn. Sorry about my associate. Best wishes to you." I walk away. Tom follows.

After speaking with the driver of the milk truck and another driver who'd witnessed the collision, I'm still angry with Brian. I stomp through the chocolate milk and dirty snow back to the embankment. I sidestep my way down the hill but lose my footing on a slippery patch of snow and finish my trek down the hill on my butt. I try to stand up right away, but I slip again, this time falling forward. My pants are soaking wet. My hands are muddy, and I've lost a shoe. My day keeps getting better.

Brian arrives first at the scene of *my accident* which surprises me since he'd left my shadow after trying to mess up my interview with Quinn, his reporter's notebook hanging out of his back pocket. He doesn't hold in his laughter as he jogs down the hill behind me. "You really know how to make an exit," he says. "Here, grab my hand." He reaches his hand out to me.

I slap it away and accept Tom's help when he's rejoined us after filming more images but not shots with Brian in them. "Are you okay, Meg?" he asks, pulling me to my feet.

"I'm fine," I say too cheerily, "Nothing damaged!"

"But how's your ego?" Brian asks as he hands me my shoe.

"My *ego* is solid though not as large as yours." I stomp through the dirty snow as quickly as I can to get back to the van first and grab hold of the passenger door. Tom throws me an old towel for the front seat, and I slam the door shut behind me before Brian can reply. Still, I have to give it to Brian to find another way to get the story even when the cameraman had taken my side for the day. We don't talk all the way back to the station.

"Send the tape to editing," Jerry says when I walk into the station. "We're going to run it on the 5:30 news. What took you guys so long?" he asks before seeing my muddy clothes. "What happened to you, Meg?" His eyes are as big as teacup saucers. Jerry is a great boss. Part of being a great boss it making sure things are done right and on time. And *without incident,* his favorite phrase when out on assignment.

"She bruised her bum, apparently, but not her ego, Jerry. This one's a tough cookie," Brian says gleefully.

I glare at him.

"Jerry, I have the best stories to tell," says Brian.

I purse my lips and stare at Brian. He's smiling so widely that his perfect teeth look like they'll pop out of his mouth with one swing.

"You went on camera?" Jerry asks, raising an eyebrow in surprise and ignoring my appearance for a moment.

"Well, actually I like to talk to my sources *off camera* first. Then I record my reflections on camera when I get back to the station. The camera intimidates sources from talking when they've been through something traumatic," he says, smiling as fake as the eyelashes on a Hollywood starlet.

I want to vomit from the acridness of his words. Plus, I really want to clean up and change clothes.

"So, I think I'll use the stationary camera I saw in the back offices to record my segment for tonight's news."

"That is ridiculous!" I can't hold back. "Jerry, I have a witness on camera who gave me an awesome interview. I talked to the driver of the milk truck. That's all we need along with Tom's shots of the scene. This isn't a major story, after all. We don't need Brian to do *anything*."

Jerry looks between Brian and me. I know he's weighing his options—keeping me happy and accommodating the new guy. "Hmm...Brian, go ahead and record your piece. Meg, take Brian's segment to editing with your segment." He sighs and curses under his breath. "You know I'm not happy about this. It's going to put us right up to news time. You are both making my job harder. If you learn to play nicely, things will be a lot easier for *all* of us." He walks away a few steps before adding. "You have 45 minutes. No exception. And clean yourself up, Meg! You look a mess!"

I death stare at Brian who has the audacity to laugh out loud. "If you play nice, you get what you want. You heard Jerry, Meg. Seems like you need to learn how to be nice. Grab a drink with me tonight, and I'll teach you how to be nice." He winks at me.

"I'd rather drink alone for the rest of my life than ever go out with you."

He snorts out loud and covers his mouth with a sickening giggle. "*That,* my dear, is not a stretch to imagine. Enjoy your solitude."

"You have fifteen minutes to get your part to me or the editing department won't have time to mesh it with mine!" I spit out before Brian saunters away.

I watch him walk away to record his story—my story—and dream about taking off my low black pump and throwing it at his head.

Marcy Blesy is the author of over thirty books including the popular cozy mystery series: The Tucson Valley Retirement Community Cozy Mystery Series. Her adult romance mystery series includes The Secret of Blue Lake and The Secret of Silver Beach, set in Michigan. Her children's books include the bestselling Be the Vet Series along with the following early chapter book series: Evie and the Volunteers, Niles and Bradford, Third Grade Outsider, and Hazel, the Clinic Cat. Her picture book, Am I Like My Daddy?, helps children who experienced the loss of a parent when they were young.

Marcy enjoys searching for treasures along the shores of Lake Michigan. She's still waiting for the day when she finds a piece of red beach glass. By day she teaches creative writing virtually to amazing students around the world.

Marcy is a believer in love and enjoys nothing more than making her readers feel a book more than simply reading it.

I would like to extend a heartfelt thanks to Betty for being the first person to read The Tucson Valley Retirement Community cozy mysteries and for giving me her guidance and expertise as my editor. Her personal pep talks are always welcome.

Thank you to Ed, Connor, and Luke for always championing my dreams and for believing in me. Thank you to Tom, Cheryl, and Megan for being such supports with my writing and in life.

And, finally, I'd like to think that my *Golden Girls* and *Murder She Wrote*-loving mom is smiling down on me, and perhaps, reading over my shoulder. Love you, Mom.

Young Adult Historical Fiction:

War and Me

Amazon Reviewer: *The story and characters draw you in. I felt like I was in the story and feeling the emotions of each character. I laughed. I cried. I couldn't put the book down! The story takes place during the WW2 era and intertwines love with the realities of war. A must read!*

Flying model airplanes isn't cool, not for fifteen-year-old girls in the 1940's. No one understands Julianna's love of flying model airplanes but her dad. When he leaves to fly bomber planes in Europe forcing Julianna to deal with her mother's growing depression alone, she feels abandoned until she meets Ben, the new boy in town. But when he signs up for the war, too, she has to consider whether letting her first love drift away would be far easier than waiting for the next casualties.

Children's Chapter Books:

Be the Vet Series

Evie and the Volunteers Series

Niles and Bradford Series

Clara and Tuni Series

Third Grade Outsider Series

Hazel, the Clinic Cat, Series

Made in United States
North Haven, CT
27 July 2024